Personal Appearances Are Everything

Personal Appearances Are Everything

◆

Bitty Collins
Carolyn Jaxson

Dear Nelson,
Enjoy ♡
Carolyn Jaxson
+
Bitty Collins

FIRST EDITION

Printed in the United States of America

Cover design by Robert R. Belanger

ISBN-13: 978-1729874578
ISBN-10: 1729874576

Acknowledgments

We could not have completed this book without the support of our family and friends. Lemmy and Jaxson, your love and patience helped us persevere. Without the wine, sweets and snacks, we never would have finished! We would also like to thank Jessica, Anita, Elizabeth, KPH, and Tom for reading our first draft. Know that we took your notes to heart. Rob, thank you for designing our book cover. There is no one better. And, of course, many thanks for the continued support of our retail family. You know who you are.

Prologue

The magnificent crystal-blue ocean is off the coast of somewhere sunny. Maybe California or Florida. Wherever the place might be, it is a still and peaceful refuge, a place of tranquility and hope. Seagulls glide gracefully over the horizon, occasionally swooping down to skim the surface. In this calm, beautiful world, where the sun always shines down and magnifies the heavenly waters, it appears that this perfection cannot be disrupted. That is, unless you plunge below the surface... to the dark depths that are home to the tens of thousands of exotic species where only the strongest survive. These sea creatures survive in extreme conditions.

Among them, alone in the bowels of the sea, swims a single, beautifully colored fish, slowly moving along without a care in the world. Helpless, vulnerable, in this cavernous blue-grey surrounding, the little fish must move quickly if it is to survive. Can this fish make it to safety?

It is too late. A massive steel-grey shark comes into view. The predator is in sight. The deadliest of all sea creatures. This is the Great White, otherwise known as... White Death. The little fish freezes, then struggles to swim away. It is panicking as death draws near, and does not stand a chance. Suddenly, a baby shark comes in to view, trapping the fish. With great aggression, both sharks attack the little fish, ripping its turquoise, orange and rose-colored gills apart until nothing is left but small clouds of blood that rise up into the endless blue. It only took ten seconds for the Great White to devour its prey!

◆

Suddenly Mary woke up, clutching her stomach and in a state of absolute panic. Her nightgown was drenched in perspiration. *Oh my gosh, it was just a dream.*

Her nerves were getting the better of her, the anticipation of getting her very first job in the fast-paced world of luxury. Mary looked at her phone to check what time it was. *Only 5:00am.* There was no way that she could fall back to sleep now. Not after that terrifying dream and a night of anxious tossing and turning.

It was exciting as well as nerve wracking the thought of being hired at the prestigious HeidtMoore department store. She had just graduated from community college with a degree in Fashion Marketing. She could spend a year or so at the HeidtMoore, then go on to work for a fashion magazine or even a luxury designer. It would be an amazing stepping stone into the world of luxury and opulence.

True, Mary didn't come from money or have social connections, like so many of the beautiful people who worked in fashion. She also didn't have any sales experience. But she had ambition and, if she could show them how driven she was to succeed, surely they would give her a chance. She would do anything to get her foot in the door. This wasn't just any old retail job she had applied for after all. No, this was working for the HeidtMoore... the finest and most prestigious department store in the country, if not the world! Could she do it? Was she good enough?

Mary started to doubt herself. She'd already made it through two interviews over the phone and passed all of the drug tests, which wasn't exactly hard, given the fact that the only alcohol Mary had ever tasted was a sip of Barefoot sparkling wine to celebrate her First Communion and a few cocktails during college. But so far, so good. The questions were a breeze.

Today, though, was the final test, the day of reckoning: her final meeting with Human Resources, where someone would tell her if the job was hers or not.

Since Mary was a child, she had heard and read stories about all of the famous people who held personal appearances or who simply shopped at the HeidtMoore for their luxury brands: Rolex, Cartier, Chanel, and other names that she came to know from flipping through the pages of *Vogue* and *Harper's Bazaar*. Mary would pass the time reading them and the latest magazines while she waited for her mother, Deloris, to finish up with her last clients at the hair salon.

Mary and Deloris would often go to the HeidtMoore to stand outside the renowned department store, peering through the enormous glass windows at the magnificent larger-than-life displays. Each windowpane portrayed a story, enticing shoppers into the store. There was a Tsarina running toward her lover, an imperial king, and also an English tea party with live exotic animals roaming about as guests. This was always Mary's favorite, although she often wondered how they managed to keep the tiger from eating any of the expensively dressed mannequins that were propped up at the garden table. It was quite simply a mystery and that was all part of the store's allure.

At Christmastime, the two loved to visit the store for its annual tree lighting ceremony, where complimentary hot chocolate was served in special eighteen-carat gold cups, one-of-a-kind keepsakes that each customer could take home.

Mary and Deloris never actually set foot inside the store. Deloris forbid them from going in for fear that it would be frowned upon, as she felt inadequate limping about with a cane and having her daughter help her around everywhere. But the real reason that she did not step into the HeidtMoore was the fear of running into Mr. Heidt himself.

"Mama. Just once, let's just go in and look. What's the worst that can happen?" Mary would plead.

"*Mi amor*, we don't belong in there. Let's go now." And off they would go, Mary trying to hide her disappointment as her mother's insecurity closed off all forms of communication on the matter. Now, not only was Mary finally getting to go into the department store, but if things went as she planned, she would be a member of its elite society.

The formidable HeidtMoore, was an exclusive and glamorous Mecca for fashionistas, society figures and movie stars. Its five-story façades were famous for their architectural elegance, with a marble and limestone design that took years to build and front doors that were made of pure gold. The interiors attracted tourists from around the world, throngs of whom came to view the magnificent $80-million-dollar spiral escalator, built in the center of the store and winding five stories around the largest public fish tank in the world.

Mr. Heidt, Sr., the founder and CEO, provided a beautiful yet exclusive gateway for the everyday consumer to the magical and mystical world of high fashion and couture. Mr. Heidt had been a very kind and wise man. He was completely selfless, despite his wealth and celebrity. He was also a very shrewd and powerful businessman. Above all, he founded his company upon the idea that shopping was an "experience," not a chore, and that whatever a customer wanted or needed could be found in one building, under one roof. He wanted the customer to feel transported into another world, one that they could only imagine in their dreams. He had set out to create a slice of heaven on earth and it was a goal that he had worked hard to achieve. If a client needed a last-minute alteration for an outfit to be worn that same day and couldn't get to the store, it wasn't a problem. HeidtMoore would dispatch a seamstress to get the job done. If a client needed to find organic food consisting of beans found only in South America (a fad during one particular season), the HeidtMoore could do it. Even if it meant flying a private plane to the client's villa in the Mediterranean to make the delivery, the HeidtMoore would make sure it was handled. If a Saudi-Arabian princess wanted to close the store for a few hours so that her ten friends could shop in privacy, the HeidtMoore would be there to accommodate her. Anybody who was anybody knew and loved the HeidtMoore. It was a place where every customer, no matter who they were or where they came from, was waited on hand and foot. There was nothing that the store wouldn't do to satisfy its customers and there was no price too high.

Perhaps the most classic example of the HeidtMoore's level of exclusivity was experienced by Lord and Lady Dingle. These minor aristocrats were visiting from England and discovered that they had not brought a priceless gift that they had handpicked for a former President of the United States. Their maid had forgotten to pack it and when Lady Dingle found out that it was still back in London, she fainted. The Dingles had put their last penny into the expensive, handmade mahogany riding crop and even had the initials *L.B.J.* engraved on the gold handle.

"Gawd! Darling, the riding crop's gone missing!" Lady Dingle shrieked.

"I'll call the HeidtMoore. They'll know what to do!" And like a hippopotamus about to eat a buzzing insect, Lord Dingle opened his mouth as wide as it could go and threw in a fistful of the peanuts that he'd found in the mini bar. The very next morning, a courier arrived at the hotel with a beautifully wrapped package. Lady Dingle found a note just inside the box on Crane stationary.

It is a great pleasure to be at your service. We sincerely hope this gift will satisfy the giver as well as the recipient.

With gratitude,
Mr. Heidt, Store Manager

The gift was an exact replica of the riding crop that they had left behind. *The HeidtMoore really did work miracles.* The crop lay inside a gold box in perfectly crisp white tissue paper, polished to perfection and immaculate. They couldn't have gotten better service at Harrods or Harvey Nichols, or Bergdorf's for that matter. After that, Lord and Lady Dingle made it a point to visit the store regularly. Sometimes they visited the country just to go the HeidtMoore.

That was in the beginning, many years before the reins were given to Mr. Heidt's son. Mr. Heidt, Jr., had become CEO during the 1980s. Similar to his father, he had good business savvy. But his major flaw, the one that kept him in trouble, was his love of women. It was said by many in both the fashion and retail industries that getting to work for Mr. Heidt, Jr. was akin to being given the golden keys to all of the great fashion houses: Givenchy, Valentino, Lanvin, and others. Even the grand editors-in-chief of magazines like *Vogue* would often seek Mr. Heidt's opinion before any editorial was put in print.

♦

Mary jumped out of bed and raced to the shower... only to find her ten-year-old brother, Samson, blocking the door.

"What are you doing? I have to get in. Come on! Let me in. *Please.*" Mary reasoned with the plump and freckled little boy standing in front of her.

"Yeah, yeah. I don't think so...," Samson said, folding his pudgy arms in front of him.

Oh no. He's working on another one of his "experiments." Mary hoped that this was not the case. The last time Samson tried one of his magic tricks, he almost made the bathroom explode and managed to somehow singe every towel and curtain in a space the size of a broom closet.

"Can't you practice this at school? I'm sure there's a safe space for you there." Mary didn't want to patronize her brother but sometimes it was hard not to do so. He finally relented and got in the room and locked the door.

After winning the battle of the bathroom, Mary quickly showered and returned to her bedroom to finish getting ready. All she could think about was the job, the famous people she would meet, and the opportunities that would come her way. It would also be a means to an end. No more living with her bratty brother and her needy mother. Finally, Mary would be free. Free from all of the obligations and pressures of her demanding family. She did love her family, there was no doubt about that, but oh, did they stifle her! Mary was young and she was ready to conquer the world.

"Your eggy peggy is ready!" Deloris shouted up the stairwell. She still had the tendency to treat Mary like a baby. Mary had long since resigned herself to the fact that this would always be the case. It wasn't worth putting up a fight and trying to change her ways. She never would.

"Yes, I'll be down shortly." Mary carefully zipped up the back of her navy blue Banana Republic dress and took one last look at herself in the mirror. Satisfied with the way that she looked, she grabbed her matching blazer and headed downstairs for breakfast.

Boggs Daniel

Revving the engine of his brand-new lime-green Mercedes convertible, Boggs Daniel sped out of the driveway of his sleek, mid-century modern home in Highland Park, an affluent suburb of Dallas. Boggs was feeling good. Real good. Heidt Jr. was out of town, probably at some fashion show or something, but Boggs didn't recall details that didn't directly have to do with him or his immediate success. Oh no... Boggs had bigger fish to fry. He was right where he needed to be in his career in order to make it to the top. He still had the same enthusiasm and ambition as when he was thirty years old. *Boy, was that a long time ago.*

Back in the day, when Boggs taught cheerleading to spoiled, rich teenage girls, the world was his oyster. When the girls got older and married quarterbacks or men in oil and gas (whom they would later divorce), there were fewer applicants to take their place, so Boggs had to look to other means of employment. Then he fell into real estate. For a while, things looked very promising. He was great at making deals and earned a fabulous living from selling expensive homes. That was, until he was caught in a compromising position, literally with his pants down, on the marble floor of one of his $5 million-dollar listings. To avoid any embarrassment, he resigned that day. Not knowing what to do, he called the mother of an ex-cheerleader who still owed him a favor. Her daughter, Summer, had been one of the clumsiest girls who Boggs had ever taught. She was just awful and moved like an elephant, but her mother begged Boggs not to throw Summer off the squad. She would do anything if only he would keep her daughter. So, Boggs kept Summer on the team and resigned himself to a tortuous season of trying to teach the girl to tumble. Now it was his turn to ask for a favor. Maybe she could have a word with her family friend, Mr. Heidt, about a job? The rest was history.

It was astonishing to think that he had started his retail career selling ties. From there, Boggs became Assistant Buyer for the Ladies' Shoes department. It was a job that he liked but, ultimately, he preferred the faster pace of working in the store. He moved up to become manager of Precious Jewelry, one of the hardest managerial positions. He remained there for a few years until he finally got his big break, the one he'd been waiting for ever since he'd started at the HeidtMoore: promotion to Assistant General Manager, or AGM as it was commonly referred to. Boggs felt sure that it wouldn't be too much longer before he ran the entire operation himself. *I mean, how much longer did Mr. Heidt expect to reign? Even if he was the son of the founder, he hardly spent any time in the store anymore.* He had to retire sometime, and Boggs felt that he was the perfect replacement.

During the weeks when Mr. H., as Boggs liked to call him, would be away from the store, it would be Boggs's turn to call the shots and let 'em know who's who. He had a plan, and no one would stand in his way. Well, except for his nemesis, Sloan Garrett.

Pulling up to a stoplight, Boggs considered how Rod, his life partner of ten years, was helping with his ambition to run the HeidtMoore. Their relationship was based on unconditional love and trust. But lately something was different. Boggs started to reconsider just how loving his partner, Rod, really was. *Semi loving? Sort of loving? God damn! There was no love!* Boggs thumped the steering wheel hard out of frustration, causing the car horn to sound.

Ever since Boggs received his promotion to AGM, Rod had become needier, yet more distant. It was as if he resented Boggs being the breadwinner but, for crying out loud, Boggs had always been the one making the money! Boggs climbed the corporate ladder while Rod was free to pursue his interests that didn't pay as well, if at all. For example, since one of Rod's interests had been gardening, he decided to start a garden club for disadvantaged inner-city kids... and Boggs had to give Rod his bonus check to help start the noble venture.

It wasn't just Rod's gorgeous physique that Boggs was attracted to; it was his heart too. If Rod saw a homeless man, he would give the guy money or something to eat, be it an apple or a power bar or even his last stick of gum. He was generous to a fault. It was annoying to Boggs, particularly since Rod didn't work. But who was he to argue? Boggs had been raised in a strict Baptist family, so he could hardly go against Scripture and refuse to give money to the poor. But there was another issue too. The truth was, Rod had let himself become fat. This was very, very disturbing to Boggs, as he'd spent a small fortune on Brioni suits for his partner that now no longer fit. What happened to the cute boy who he'd first met dancing in a Speedo at a gay club? The one with the gorgeous, tan body ripped to perfection? Where was that guy? The Zegna suit that Boggs was wearing fit better than it did on Rod. It was just plain sad.

Suddenly a loud cry was heard.

"Get a move on! Christ!" screamed the disgruntled driver in the Honda behind his sleek Mercedes. The light had turned green.

"All right!" Boggs shouted back, putting his foot on the accelerator.

But he couldn't get Rod off his mind. Blocking out any negative thoughts about his predicament, Boggs put on his favorite song on the car iPad and blasted the volume. With his boundless optimism and bravado, he sang every word of the song.

"Just a small-town girl living in a lonely world...." He did not notice the stares of other drivers. Or the honking horns. He came to an intersection just as the light turned red.

"Up and down the boulevard...."

At the top of his lungs, he belted out his favorite part, *"Don't stop believin'! Streetlights, people...."*

HONK. HONK.

The light had turned green.

"Alright, alright. Take it easy." Boggs sped off.

Moments later, Boggs swerved into his designated parking spot, in the second row of the HeidtMoore's third-floor parking garage. Hoisting his whole 6-foot, 2-inch muscular body over the door frame of the car with one hand, his lanky legs narrowly missed a collision with the concrete pillar to the left of his parking spot near the stairs. But he couldn't save himself from slipping on an unforeseen plastic bottle cap laying on the ground of the cement floor.

What the...!? Getting up from the ground and brushing himself off, Boggs hoped that no one had witnessed his embarrassing fall. Or that the leg of his $2,000 pants was slightly ripped. He swung his custom-made silk-lined blazer over his shoulder.

"Hey, are you alright?" a young girl called out to him, as she was getting out of her car.

Oh, jeez....

"Yep. I'm good. Thanks." He pretended that he hadn't just grazed his knee and was trying very hard not to limp. But the act did not dissuade the young girl from coming over to make sure he was really alright.

They started walking together, much to Boggs's annoyance. *This girl wasn't going anywhere.*

"So... You work for the company? I haven't seen you around."

"Um... no. Well, I hope to. I'm here for my final interview," Mary said with a mixture of excitement and nervousness.

"Really? Good luck. This is a mighty fine place to work."

"It's what I've always wanted."

"What's your name?"

"Mary."

"Well, Mary, if you get to work here, you'll be the luckiest person on earth. We have the finest merchandise, the most sophisticated associates, the best events. You name it, we have it," Boggs said proudly.

"Wow, it really is an amazing place. And what, if you don't mind me asking, do you do?"

"Me? General Manager. Well, I mean—" But before Boggs could explain himself, Mary interrupted him.

"You are? What an honor to meet you, especially after everything I've read."

"You've read about me? I didn't know there was that much out there."

"Oh yes, lots. You're an idol."

"We should grab coffee sometime. I like the way you talk." Suddenly the faint sound of Lady Gaga's *Born This Way* became louder. "I can tell already that you're gonna go far," Boggs said as he pulled out his phone. Tapping a button, the ringtone stopped, and he put the phone up to his ear. "You go ahead. I gotta take this."

Mary was thrilled about her chance meeting with the man himself, Mr. Heidt. She was bewildered by how different he appeared in reality.

Entrance to the Wild

As Mary got closer to the employee entrance to the HeidtMoore, she could see several models walking in. *My gosh! They work here?* Mary considered walking the other way, back to her car.

Each girl who entered through those giant iron doors was at least six feet tall and dressed immaculately. They were walking fashion ads in their sky-high Valentino rock-stud shoes and imaginatively coordinated designer outfits.

One of the girls, Mary noticed, was dressed in Dolce & Gabbana from head to toe. The baby-pink gingham pencil skirt, paired with a sheer, long-sleeve silk fuchsia blouse, would have looked obscene on anyone else but on her it looked spectacular. Mary recognized the outfit from a cover story about the Italian design duo in *Elle* magazine that she'd read just a few weeks ago. It was amazing to see their ensemble in real life.

There was another girl, just as pretty as the last, wearing a Chanel jacket. *No way! Was that real?* Of course, it had to be real. This was the HeidtMoore, after all. Mary felt sure that she'd seen the jacket in *Allure*… or was it *Vogue*? The black and white boucle jacket must have cost more than the mortgage on her mother's house. Did the HeidtMoore really pay that well or was the employee discount that ridiculously good?

Like elegant giraffes, one after the other, each girl sauntered in, Mary hoped that they would not see her. I mean, she could take judgment and even expected it if the job were to become hers, but she just didn't want it on this day of all days.

One of the drop-dead gorgeous girls had stopped, blocking the doorway. Why would she do that? Looking at her size-2 frame in the colorful, short, designer frock and long blond hair—*was that really natural?*—made Mary feel increasingly shabby, like she dressed herself in a potato sack. *Gosh, it was too late now.* Her meeting was in fifteen minutes. She looked boring, drab and old in comparison to the bright young things walking into the HeidtMoore. It was mortifying. Mary had to walk past the tall creature blocking the door. It felt like junior high school all over again. *It was now or never.* She had to barge through and overcome her fear. What was the worst that could happen? The giraffe-like model would spit on her? Or punch her for not carrying the latest designer bag? No. Of course not! *This was a department store, not an insane asylum!* The epitome of civilized behavior... or so she thought.

Mary marched through, head held high, and chose to ignore the stormy stare coming her way. She did notice, however, that the beautiful girl happened to be wearing the biggest diamond ring that Mary had ever seen. The rock sparkled so brightly that it was blinding; for a split-second, Mary felt off balance. Holding her breath and charging on, Mary walked past the gleaming gemstone and headed through a narrow grey hallway.

At the very end of the bleak looking hallway was a man sitting behind a desk. He looked like a drill sergeant. He was very handsome, in a Vin Diesel sort of way, a Latino man with biceps the size of watermelons and a no-nonsense attitude. Mary could tell that he must work out a lot.

"Welcome. Sign in, please," he said, in a deep, husky voice.

"Sure. Out of curiosity, who were those girls that walked through?"

"Buyers. They come in every so often. Yep. Holier than thou," he replied, raising his eye brows. "Why? They give you any hassle?"

"No. Not at all. Just curious. It's fine," Mary said, trying to hide her insecurity. She noticed two other men in the back of an office behind him. The one named Brad was eating a burrito. He nodded at Mary then turned to one of the TV screens next to him. *They must also be with store security.*

"They give you grief, you come see me, alright?" Mary noticed that he puffed out his chest when he said this. Typically, Mary was turned off by this sort of thing. But for some reason, she found him slightly endearing. He had gorgeous brown eyes and she had to admit she did find his voice very sexy. The muscles too. So big that they bulged through his shirt, making it even tighter than it already was. She guessed that he must be the head of Security.

"Please write your name and what department you work in on this sheet of paper."

"I don't work in any department. I'm here for an interview."

"What job are you applying for? Hope it's not in Children's, for your sake."

Amused by this suggestion, Mary laughed. "No way! Children are *not* my thing. I'm hoping to be in Fine Apparel."

"Good. Well, good luck."

"Thanks. How do I get to HR?"

"Ok. So...." Mary swore that she saw him flexing a muscle, as he pointed down the hall. "Whatever you do, don't take the stairs. You'll never get there. It's a maze. Go down this hallway here, get to the swinging doors, you'll be in Cosmetics, take a right at Estée, go 'til you see Tom Ford, then take another right, and an immediate left at Bobbi Brown. You'll see the elevator right in front. Best catch that. It leads straight to the office."

"I see. Yes, I'm sure I'll find it. Thanks," Mary said, with a slight hesitation.

"Got it?"

Mary nodded yes, obediently. "Good. My name is Ignacio, but people call me Nacho, by the way."

"Nacho. Thank you so much." Mary did as she was told, trying hard to remember the exceedingly complicated directions.

She proceeded down the long, dark hallway, passing gossiping sales associates who were rushing in for work, frantically punching the time clock that greeted them as they arrived for their shifts. Mary noticed the motivational motifs that were plastered on either side of the hallway walls. It reminded Mary of Kindergarten. *"Make today the best day"* was written in giant letters cut out of brightly colored construction paper.

On another wall was an employee recognition board. Mary glanced at the customer note beside the picture of a smiling associate: *"Dear Mr. Heidt, I was in a panic until DeeDee, in handbags, SAVED my life. You see, I have been a very loyal customer for 40 years...."* And on the letter went. Mary couldn't imagine what the circumstances could have been to receive a letter like that, but she couldn't stop to finish reading it. She couldn't afford to be late.

♦

Not far behind Mary, Boggs was bounding in through the employee entrance. He saw Nacho and the glum-looking security team.

"Mornin' team. It's gonna be a great day. C'mon, it ain't so bad! Turn that frown upside down."

"Not sure about that, Mr. Boggs. The computers are down, so no email from the server. AGAIN." Nacho was exasperated.

"C'mon! What, no email from the server? Did you call the I.T. department?"

"Yes, of course we did. I couldn't get through. I'll try again in a moment."

"Ya see? Ya got this, kid. Why ya stressin'? Hey, by the way, how much did we do yesterday in the store? I know that we had a major Precious

Jewelry sale."

"That's just it! It's in the email. I won't have it until the server is fixed. I've tried, Mr. Boggs, I've tried."

"Try harder! Does Mr. H know about this?

"Nope, he's M.I.A." Nacho's phone rang. Boggs took this as his cue to leave.

"Hi. This is Nacho. Yes, you are calling the HeidtMoore. Help Desk, thank you for returning my call! We don't have email. That's right. Mind if I put you on speaker?"

The voice at the other end had a thick Indian accent and the reception wasn't good, which made it difficult to hear. But Nacho had to multitask. There was a store to open and he needed to make sure each floor was ready and secure for the day ahead.

"Thank you for calling. I shall help you the very, very best I can. My name is Raj Agnihotri."

"That's great, Raj. So, like, can you get the server running again?" A crackling sound was heard over the phone line.

"What? I cannot understand. Sorry, breaking up." The crackling sound got louder, forcing Nacho to speak clearer.

"We need to have the server up and running. No email! Can you hear me?"

"Ah, yes. Better now. I am sorry for that inconvenience."

"Right. Can you tell us how long it will take?"

"What did you say? I am sorry I do not know what you mean. Can you speak up, please?"

"I said, 'how long will it take?' We need to have the SERVER UP AND RUNNING!"

"¿*Comprende*?" Brad chimed in.

"Er, wrong language." Brad shrugged and went back to monitoring the screens before him.

"What is it that you want me to do?" Raj inquired innocently.

"Fix. The. Server!"

"Your voice is breaking up. Can you repeat?" Nacho picked up the phone and spoke into the receiver.

"NO server. NO email. NO sales for the store."

"You need email for sales? You are selling email? I am sorry. I do not understand."

"We need the server up, to.... Can you just fix it!?" The line went staticky and all Nacho could hear was Raj thanking him for his call. *Unbelievable.* The line went dead and Nacho slammed the phone down. It had been a hell of a morning.

"Don't worry bro. At least you met a cute girl this morning," said Brad, not helping the situation.

"What? I didn't even notice. What cute girl? There was a cute girl?" Nacho felt the heat rise up his cheeks.

"For real? The new girl here for her interview. You guys were cute."

"I'd never date an employee. Out of the question."

"Yeah we noticed how 'accommodating' you were. If I didn't have a girl, I'd go for her." Nacho couldn't help but smile despite himself.

"Hey. Enough. We got a job to do. Brad, I'd like you to keep calling India and get the systems working again. Danny, I want you to keep an eye on the fifth and third floors. Keep an eye on Olga. Make sure she's following the opening procedures. Got it?"

"Got it," Brad and Danny responded in unison. They were good guys, if a little dim.

◆

Mary walked through the swinging doors at the end of the hallway, which opened into the incredibly huge cosmetics department of the store. It was wild, a sharp contrast to the sterile employee entrance, Mary stood in awe of what she saw before her. It was incredible. Everything was bright and dazzling. She stopped to marvel at the color palettes, lipsticks, bronzers, brushes, lipsticks, and eye shadows at the many counters scattered around the department. Mary moved on to another counter, then another and another, distracted by the products before her. There was every color and shade imaginable. And every sort of other gimmick to suck in, reduce and eliminate cellulite from whatever part of the body one so desired. *This place was overwhelming.* Each one of the cosmetic bays on the floor provided a color, treatment, or enhancer that promised to stop the aging process.

"Hiiii, honey. My first customer of the day. Let me put some of this revitalizing cream on your hand. Not that you look old. It's just putting this on will make you look like a Kendall Jenner. Hold out your hand." The woman speaking to her was wearing a long black lace skirt and brown suede cowboy jacket, and must have been at least seventy years old.

"No thank you. I'm going to HR. Can you tell me where that is please?" As soon as Mary mentioned HR the woman walked away, no longer interested. Mary stood there, stunned by the lack of helpfulness.

"She's such an old witch. Her name is Shirley. Pay no attention. My name is Zane. I'll take you to HR. I have to go there anyway. I'm in trouble again," said a young man who had more bronzer on his face than could be imagined.

"Thanks, I appreciate it. Shirley works for the company?" Mary said incredulously.

"Are you kidding? In her dreams! She's what we call a 'vendor.'"

"Oh? What's that?"

"You're obviously not working in Cosmetics," Zane said with a sarcastic undertone. He went on to explain. "A vendor is someone who gets paid to freelance and come into the store when it suits them. They are the lowlifes of the world, the bottom-feeders out to make a quick buck or marry rich." Thinking that this was a little harsh, Mary decided to keep her mouth shut.

Zane continued, "We'll take this. I loathe the freight. Only for housekeeping." Mary and Zane passed the infamous fish tank and stepped onto the winding escalator going up. Mary looked right and suddenly found herself eye-to-eye with the shark. Zane laughed. He was clearly enjoying every moment teaching his latest victim the ways of retail.

Zane turned to look back at the Cosmetics floor below. "Oh look, there's another one. She's the worst. She seems sweet but she's a shark. She'll stop at nothing to make a sale... or to steal a client."

Mary turned to see who he was talking about. She saw a woman dressed in a sailor suit with a Peter Pan collar and a tilted sailor hat. Not even the ginormous mound of foundation caked on her face could conceal the deep lines, no doubt a living testament to the years of selling her wares on the cosmetics floor of the HeidtMoore. Her ruby-red lips were lined with a deeper shade, verging on plum. She was a spectacle and Mary couldn't take her eyes off her.

"Shit! My customer is here. Gotta run. Good luck up there." Zane immediately ran up the moving stairs, in front of Mary, and jumped on the one going down, leaving Mary to find her way on her own.

"Wait! Where am I going?"

But Zane had already moved on and out of sight.

♦

Brandi was perusing the racks of expensive designer dresses on sale on the third floor. She had a little time since her interview wouldn't be there for another ten minutes. As Human Resources Assistant Manager, Brandi had the important job of interviewing every candidate for the HeidtMoore. At just 32 years old, she was young to hold such a position within the company. She had been working at the store since graduating from college. With her dirty blond hair and long, lacquered pink fingernails, she wasn't necessarily a reflection of the chic and stylish store. Her clothing always had a synthetic quality and her plastic heels were never fewer than 6 inches tall. She gave—and indeed encouraged—fun and her bubbly personality was perfect for her HR role. For the most part, everyone liked Brandi, particularly Chef.

"Brandi! Hey, Brandi!" Chef called over to her from across the department.

She was pleased to see him. "Hi, Chef! How are you? What is the special today? I walked by earlier, to talk about employment openings, and something smelled so good."

"You wanna know what smells good?" Chef actually went by "Chef" as no one seemed to remember his name. He was a 45-year-old burly, tattooed cook from New Jersey. He was tough, and his confidence bordered on arrogance.

Brandi looked around to make sure no one was watching their slightly flirty interlude. She smiled.

"Why don't you tell me... *Chef.*"

"So, I gotta new recipe I'm tryin'. Wanna taste?" She was tempted but couldn't be late for her interview. Should she do it? Was it worth it? Frank would go nuts if she wasn't back in time. *He was such a micromanaging lunatic.*

"Sure. Ten minutes?"

"Great. Don't worry. It won't take longer than that. Trust me."

◆

Customers were starting to pour into the store, spreading out in every direction. Mary stepped out onto the second floor, literally falling into the world of handbags and accessories. Hundreds of exotic bags, made of crocodile, python, and animals that Mary had never even heard of. There were countless boutiques. Gucci, Fendi, Chanel, and Louis Vuitton were just a few of the shops that made up the expansive floor that seemed to Mary to be the size of a football field. Immediately, Mary was approached by a sales associate.

"I help you. I help you. Good. They all good bags." A small, plump woman with short dyed-black hair and a thick Russian accent rushed up to Mary.

"Actually, I'm looking for HR." Mary hoped that she might find the direction she needed.

"Why HR?" inquired the Russian.

"I have an interview." The Russian wasn't listening though.

"You come with me. HR no good. You see this bag? You like? Gimme pen. Come on. Gimme. I write down name and you come back later. For bag," the Russian said, picking up an orange ostrich bag.

Taking out a gold pen from her purse. "Listen, I actually have an interview. I really need to—"

Offended by Mary's lack of enthusiasm, the Russian snapped back. "What! You don't like? How could be you don't like? But this Prada! Or maybe you like LV instead?"

"No really, I have to go." Mary broke away from the clutches of the mad Russian and decided that the best bet was to keep on moving. It was no time to worry about offending associates whom she might not ever see again.

"But I get you very good deal! I write down name. My name Olga. I see you again! Yah?" Mary hoped that this would not be the case. Forgetting to take back the antique pen which her mother had given to her on her sixteenth birthday, Mary quickly broke away.

Interview

It had taken Mary an additional fifteen minutes to get to Human Resources. Until this point, every interview had been via phone and Skype and Mary could understand why. It took forever to get through the departments.

After a few wrong turns, Mary made it to an office suite situated in the furthest regions of the store. A little out of breath, Mary approached the lady at the desk.

"Hello. My name is Mary. I am so sorry that I'm late."

Moments later, Brandi came out to greet her.

"Hello. My name is Brandi. Don't worry about being late. I was a bit late too. It happens all the time! So glad you could make it. It's nice to finally meet you. Would you like a coffee or some water?"

"Oh, no thank you."

"No? Okay so let's get started. First, I want you to meet with Boggs, one of our AGMs. He's really awesome. I have to finish up something."

A few minutes later, Brandi was running back to the kitchen. "Back for dessert?" said Chef, with a salacious grin across his face.

♦

In Mr. Boggs's office, Mary sank into one of the two dark-green wingback chairs. Her whole body sank in to the deep cushions. As comfortable as it was, she could tell a spring had sprung.

Boggs walked in. "Nice to see you again. So, Mary, let's get right to it."

Boggs jumped right to the chase. *Did Mr. Heidt go by Boggs? This was very odd.* Mary didn't care. All she wanted was the job.

He continued. "Why do you want to work at the HeidtMoore?" Without missing a beat, Mary smiled and took a deep breath and then told him about how much she loved people. She could tell the more that she spoke of her people skills, the more he stroked his chin, indicating that she must be on the right track.

It was Boggs's turn now. He told her at great length about what it takes to work in such a high-volume, high-powered store like the HeidtMoore. As Boggs was getting further into his endless dissertation on the high-end retail experience, Mary noticed a peculiar array of framed photographs on a shelf behind his head.

In one photograph, there was a cheerleading squad. It had obviously been taken in the late 1970s judging by the flip hairstyles of the girls and the discoloration of the photo. The one man in the picture bore a resemblance to Boggs, except that he had an Afro. *Was the serious man clad in an expensive suit in front of her an ex-cheerleader with an Afro?* It boggled her mind. She also noticed the strange and mismatched furniture in the room, which could lead someone to believe that whoever was responsible for decorating the offices had gone to a resale shop and purchased whatever they could find at random. It was more 1985 than the present day. It was strange how luxurious the entire store was but beneath its luster was a suite of grimy, dusty and outdated offices for the executive team.

"Do you have any questions?" Boggs asked Mary, distracting her from her thoughts. Mary had read a magazine an article about the five best questions to ask a future employer.

"What do you see as your biggest challenge in a store this size?"

"I like the way you think, Mary. Good question. You know I manage 1,000 employees. Yep. That's right. The store is a beast, some say it's a real zoo here. But you know what I tell myself? I say, 'Boggs, everyone is an individual. Everyone has a talent, a gift.' So, I encourage my employees to express that gift, whatever it might be, and to do their best."

Somewhat unsure of where he was going with this, Mary wondered if there was a hidden message. Gifts? What did he mean, what did that have to do with her question? The magazine didn't give her any responses to the five greatest questions. *Too bad.* How was she meant to respond when she didn't know what he was going on about? She nodded in an agreement and looked appropriately serious and thoughtful.

"Let me pose this question to you, Mer... mind if I call you 'Mer'?"

"I... okay." No one ever called her "Mer." In fact, she couldn't stand it when they did. What was wrong with Mary? It wasn't difficult to say. Two syllables. Easy. But who was she to argue?

"What would you do if you discovered a $20,000 pair of women's Moonboots went missing?" Boggs leaned back in his swivel chair, pleased with this ridiculous question.

"I... Moonboots? As in, what you wear in the snow?"

"Not just in the snow, Mer. Everyday. To the grocery store, to the gas station… okay, maybe not to the gas station," he continued, "to church."

"Right. Well… I would probably go straight to the Ladies' Shoes department and check all of the pending orders. Talk to the manager. See if anyone had returned the missing… snow boots." *Was this a trick question?* Mary had to wonder.

"Smart. You'll go far. We need someone like you making good choices."

"Oh. Thank you." Mary was flattered.

"This is what I need you to do. Take a seat outside. I need to make a call." With some effort, Mary rose from the sprung seat that she was sitting in and walked outside, closing the door halfway after her. Once she had left, Boggs dialed the store operator.

"Operator speaking," said the nasally voice at the other end. Her tone was slow and deliberate.

"Operator!" Boggs's voice boomed toward the phone, as if the operator was in a different country. "Get me Ladies' Shoes!"

"One moment. Let me connect you to—"

"Yep. Thank you!" Boggs, cutting her off, hoping that it would increase the operator's sense of urgency. It didn't.

"Thank you for your call and have a lovely day." There was no change in her delivery.

After a moment, Boggs was finally connected.

"Hey, this is Boggs. I was thinking, have we checked the pending orders on the Moonboots? Check and get back to me."

Hanging up the receiver and quickly picking it back up again, Boggs dialed another number. "Brandi! Boggs here. Hey, we gotta hire this Mary girl."

◆

Brandi had been back in her pink and glitter decorated office for less than two minutes when Mary entered to resume her interview.

"So, the position that we have for you is a sales manager position, where you will be responsible for overachieving sales goals and managing a team of nine associates. We expect all of our sales managers to meet their goals. This department usually has a plan of around $5 million annually."

"That's great. Yes, I feel very confident that I will be able to achieve goals and manage a team. Absolutely. I've helped manage my mother's hair salon and she has a staff of ten, thirteen if you include the washers and the cleaner."

"Awesome. And what would you say has been your most challenging customer service experience?"

"I would say this one time when a lady in the salon didn't like the color and said that her hair broke off. She then sent me her hair in the mail."

"Oh my gosh, that's awful. What did you do with the hair?"

"I filed it away with other customer issues and then provided the customer with a complimentary service. She was fine after that."

"Good. Compassion. You can empathize with people."

"Oh yes, definitely."

"That's great. Well, we want to offer you the job."

"You do?!"

"We think you would be perfect for our new opening. Of course, you'll have to meet with Frank briefly. He's our head of HR. I'll introduce you to him in a moment."

"Really? Oh yes, I'd love to take the position." Mary was eager and curious to know where in the store this department was.

"It's one of the smaller departments, but there's always a chance for a promotion." Brandi took a moment to take a drink from her pink Yeti flask. *Gulp.* "What do you think?"

"Yes, thank you. Oh my gosh, I've been so excited about the possibility of working here."

"Great! You'll be in Children's."

"Children's!? I don't really know about…." Brandi looked at Mary quizzically.

Brandi's tone became sharp instantly. "If you don't want it, there are a thousand other candidates who do."

"Oh, I do. I do!" Mary was a terrible liar. The truth was that Mary didn't like children. At all. They were annoying and demanding and especially after taking care of her brother, Mary had been put off of them for life. What on earth was she going to do selling clothing for rich infants?

"May I see the Children's department?"

"Of course. Let's go see Frank, then we'll walk over."

♦

Brandi asked Mary to wait for a moment and bounced off into her boss's office. There, a disgruntled old man sat looking at his computer screen, frown in place, slowly moving his computer mouse with one hand as he used the other to eat from a bag of Cheetos.

"Boggs should have called. I just met with him and we are so very happy about this new girl, Mary. This is amazing. Finally, we have a candidate who isn't a psycho."

Not being one for many words, her boss said nothing. He barely raised an eyebrow. Brandi continued, "Good. Glad you approve. The other piece of news is that—"

"God damn! Fuck, fuck, fuck this fucking shit!"

Before Brandi could say boo, the man—her boss and Head of Human Resources—threw an 8-inch binder against the wall. *Whoa.*

"Should I come back later?" Brandi asked tentatively.

Silence.

Brandi was feeling very nauseous and in need of a drink. It didn't matter that it was ten o'clock in the morning. Her boss's outbursts were getting to be a frequent occurrence and it was more than Brandi could handle.

"This fucking place." *Oh boy. He was in a foul mood today.* "What do you want?" he snarled back at Brandi.

"I came in to tell you that we picked a real winner with Mary."

"Great." Without so much as a smile, he resumed his position eating Cheetos and staring at his computer screen.

"She's outside and I need you to meet her. She's great for the Children's position."

Brandi ushered Mary into his office.

"This fucking place. What do you want?"

"This is Mary."

Frank looked up from his keyboard and glared at Mary, making her feel very uncomfortable.

"He's just having a bad day," Brandi whispered to Mary.

"Who are you?"

"Mary."

"I hired you?"

Brandi stepped in.

"This is Mary. We want to hire her."

"Which department?"

"Children's."

"Ugh. That's a shitty job." He looked back to the computer screen.

Brandi nudged Mary and motioned toward the door to leave.

"I'm taking Mary on a tour of the department now."

"Fine," Frank said as he put another Cheeto into his partially closed mouth.

Brandi closed the door and turned to Mary.

"Come on, you'll love it. I'll walk you over to the department. I think that this is going to be a great fit. I do." Before they headed to the floor, Mary saw Brandi take another sip from the Yeti flask that she apparently always carried with her.

Brats

They got to the Children's department, where children were running around everywhere. This wasn't a sales job. This was babysitting spoiled brats in a department store. It wasn't too dissimilar to the day care setup at gyms, where mothers left their children in a room while they worked out for an hour.

"Isn't this awesome!?" Brandi was overly animated. Nothing about this was awesome in Mary's mind. Two five-year-olds were running between massive stuffed animals, while another child sat on the floor throwing a tantrum and banging a toy drum. The place was littered with toys. Not only would Mary have to make her sales goals while working in this chaos, but she had a feeling she'd also be spending a large portion of the time cleaning up.

Mary gazed around the department in amazement. The place was as wild as the screaming children. Aside from the giant white fluffy polar bear and other animals, Mary spotted a mini electric Hummer SUV, a Steinway piano in miniature, and a baby kitchen with pots and pans made by Le Creuset along with little stainless-steel appliances. It was enough to make Gordon Ramsay jealous. Brandi walked Mary through the department and toward the kitchen.

"Isn't that great! So cute. I love that you can give a kid a French oven. Look, did you see the little chef hat? It's handmade in France. I know it costs about $500. It comes in one size."

"Good to know. How many of those hats do you sell?" She was curious to know why on earth anyone would pay that amount for something that wouldn't last more than two minutes and that you could find at Target for $10.

"Oh, they sell like hot cakes. Ha ha! No pun intended." Then, in all seriousness, Brandi explained why. "The mini Ecole de Cuisine Alain Ducasse chef hat was designed by the great chef himself in order to encourage young children to grow up and become culinary geniuses…

just like him." She sighed, then, as an afterthought and without any hint of irony, said, "I think it's made by Dior."

While Brandi had been talking, Mary glanced at a child taking his finger out of his nose and purposely wiping it on the hat. The repetitive action was happening as fast as the spit and drool were coming out of the infant's mouth. Mary gagged.

In another corner of the Children's department, two young and exquisitely dressed mothers were sipping champagne as their children worked very hard at destroying the rest of the area. Nannies, mostly Latinas, tried their best to calm down crying babies and hysterical Burberry-wearing toddlers.

Brandi, her grin in place like the Cheshire Cat, looked at Mary.

"How soon can you start?"

♦

Mary had accepted their offer of a managerial position. Not knowing how she would fulfill her new duties, she knew it was better than nothing. She told her mother that she had gotten the job offer when she arrived home that night. Then Mary immediately went to her room and jumped on the computer. She downloaded Mr. Heidt, Sr.'s book, *Navigating the Jungle: Self-preservation in Retail*, so that she could learn as much as possible before she started her new job the following week.

It Really Is a Zoo

Mary had been at the store a week and was only now taking the grand tour. The place was massive, 200 departments within one million square feet of retail. There wasn't a place in the store that Mary hadn't seen... or so she thought. Brandi had shown her the basement, which was a large cavernous area that housed the exotic animals used for the window displays and special events. Mary couldn't see beyond the door reading "Authorized Zookeepers Only."

Shipping and Receiving was also located in the far end of the lower level. It was an area in constant motion: packaging moving in, boxes shipping out, with everyone in uniform working diligently and paying no attention to the new employee, Mary.

They then randomly went up to another floor, where she was shown a large epicurean market. While browsing at least 300 different types of cheese, truffles and foie gras, as well as hundreds of other delicacies in the expanse food hall, Brandi had slipped away. Mary spotted her at the Champagne Bar, where she seemed to be refilling her Yeti flask. Mary was starving after looking at the incredible assortment but there was no time to eat.

"Are you ready? We have a few more floors to tour." Brandi had returned.

"We do?" Mary was exhausted and trying her best to hide it. They had started at 10:00am and now it was nearly 2:30pm. They had begun in her Children's department on the fourth floor and worked their way down to the bottom floors. They passed through the vast Men's department, a masculine hub for rich men to buy their custom-made suits and smoke specially made HeidtMoore cigars. Brandi pointed out to Mary where a massive statue of Mr. Heidt, Jr. was going to be placed. Everyone was just waiting for it to be shipped over from Italy.

"It's going to be so amazing. It's made of solid gold and I heard that they are putting diamonds in for his eyes... but don't quote me. Like, so cool, right? I wish that I had one for my home." Brandi said excitedly, then continued sipping from her Yeti.

Mary was not sure how to her interpret her gaudy description of Mr. Heidt as a statue. She was distracted by the next department ahead on their tour. Her eyes met a large neon sign that said "HEAVEN or HELL."

"What is that over there?"

"Oh... just you wait!" Brandi led Mary over to the Intimates department.

They walked toward the sign and were transported into a different area. Looking left, Mary saw a lush pink and cream boutique. Very glossy, very sweet and lovely, with mannequins dressed up like 18th-century Marie Antoinettes: lots of lace and pearls, a soft color palette and very demure. The surroundings contained every imaginable delicate panty, bra, and underpinning, all made from the finest Parisian silks and Egyptian cottons.

Then, like a shock to the system, Brandi barked, "Now, look right!" Before them was the complete antithesis of what they had just seen. This was obviously Hell—quite literally—and Mary was terrified. Display mannequins were clad in black leather bustiers. A display case carried an array of whips and chains, as well as other items with uses that Mary had no idea about or why. Madonna's song *Human Nature* was playing overhead. Luckily, they did not stay for very long before moving on to the third floor.

"It's 3:30pm. Let's go and meet Frank in the Shoe department. He's expecting us."

♦

Meanwhile, on the third floor, Boggs was heading toward Ladies' Shoes, a vast designer shoe Mecca next to the Handbag department.

"How is everyone progressing with their daily sales?" Boggs said, stopping a scurrying sales associate who was barely holding onto the dozens of boxes in her hands.

"Good," said the sales associate before disappearing behind one of the large shoe shelving units. Boggs began to assemble a new delivery of Moonboots, the hottest trend of the season, on the center table.

Approaching the display table, like the military, was Frank, with Mary and Brandi trailing behind, desperately trying to keep up.

"What on earth are those?" inquired Frank, picking up a rather heavy boot. "See," he said, showing Mary. "This is the kind of shit we sell."

"They are kind of cute," Brandi giggled.

Mary laughed nervously, unsure if this comment was supposed to be funny or not. Mary could swear she could smell alcohol. It became stronger each time that Brandi leaned in to share some tidbit or anecdote about the store. If Mary didn't know any better, she would say it was vodka, or maybe tequila. But what did she know?

"Hi there, Frank. How's it going, guys?"

"Remember Boggs? Mr. Boggs and his Moonboots," Brandi giggled. "We are giving Mary a tour of the store."

Mary picked up a silver glitter, astronaut-looking NASA-sponsored Moonboot. Looking at Boggs, she said, "I see that you solved the issue with the Moonboots."

"You betcha kid. That's what I do, solve problems. Welcome to Shoes. So, you got the job! Welcome to the HeidtMoore! This is the store where miracles happen."

"You mean you aren't Mr. Heidt?" said Mary, trying to hide her disappointment. Boggs and Brandi laughed.

"As if," Frank muttered.

"Nahhh, not me." Boggs had obviously not heard Frank's snide remark. "Boggs Daniel," he said, reaching out to shake Mary's hand. "Speaking of Mr. H, is he in the store today?"

"I haven't seen him," Brandi said. She hadn't seen him in weeks.

Frank chimed in. "He couldn't come in today. Something came up."

Was Frank covering up something?

Brandi turned to her. "Mary, why don't you look around the rest of this floor? Frank and I have a meeting. Meet me in the executive offices at 5:00pm to finish up and then you can go home."

"Okay." Mary watched the two of them walk away, leaving her with Boggs and the Moonboots.

"Mer. Good luck. See you around." Then Boggs disappeared behind the shoe shelving units.

♦

Five o'clock was quickly approaching. Mary was exhausted. She couldn't believe the sheer amount of merchandise that she had discovered was carried by the HeidtMoore. And the prices were unbelievable. She wondered if this was why her mother never wanted to go into the department store. Mary decided that she would have to put in extra hours to learn about this menagerie of products and people. She headed back to the executive offices for some quick notes from Brandi before leaving for the day.

Mary waited for Brandi. She was late, and Mary wondered if she had another emergency. Little did she know, but Brandi was stuck with the most irritating interview.

◆

In Human Resources, Brandi was trying to get through as many interviews as she could, so that she could fill the quota given to her by Corporate. It was five o'clock and she was on her fifth interview. Not bad. Hopefully this one would be good.

"I have many hobbies. Many, many. Alien-spotting, drag shows and rollerblading," said Brandi's applicant at the start of the interview.

"Oh? That's great." Brandi was very good at faking optimism. In truth she couldn't care less about the potential sales associate's personal life. All that she wanted to do was fill the position in Cosmetics. With twenty open positions, she needed to hire someone soon.

"One of my hobbies, alien-spotting, is very cool. I go all over." This was one that Brandi had never heard before. *Aliens?*

"I see. Alien-spotting. Very interesting," she glanced down at the résumé in her hands to remind herself who she was talking to. She continued, "Mi Chung. That's good. Any other jobs you would like to share with me? I see that you have worked—"

"Not only that, I can count the different species. There are over fifteen and lots of people don't even know it."

"I see. Now, what about the other jobs that you've had?"

"Oh. You're funny." He gave out a high-pitched chuckle.

It wasn't often that Brandi was at a loss for words, but this really stumped her. The applicant in front of her was new to America, having literally come off the boat from China five weeks ago. This was very unusual. *Was this a Chinese thing, this alien fascination?* She was unsure how to tie aliens to the Cosmetics job that Mi Chung was applying for.

"Different species. Wow. They exist?" Brandi couldn't believe she was having this conversation.

"Of course!"

Brandi moved uncomfortably in her chair. It was time to change the subject.

"So, tell me, why do you want to work at the HeidtMoore?"

"People."

"Pardon?"

"And I love cosmetics. I know every kind of mascara there is. Chanel. YSL. Bobbi Brown."

"Yes, good. You know the brands." *This interview was not going well.* Just a typical day. "But what makes you think that you can sell cosmetics? It's one thing to know the brands but another to know how to sell them."

"Honey, I've been wearing them since I was five. I know."

Okay, that's it. Brandi had had enough. It was time for this interview to now be over.

♦

The lady behind the desk in the center of the room, not looking up from her computer, asked Mary if she wanted water while she waited. Mary declined out of fear that she might need to use the bathroom. It just occurred to her that she had gone an entire day without going. *Seriously, if I get a bladder infection, Mama will definitely make me quit.*

The executive offices were so contrary to everything else that Mary had seen. They were a place completely devoid of atmosphere. Even the potted plant sitting on the reception desk had wilted.

Brandi came rushing in, slightly disheveled.

"Oh. My. God. I'm here! Yeah!" she said, clapping her hands in excitement. Her tumbling blonde hair looked a little matted.

"Sorry. I was just finishing up an urgent email to Mr. Heidt. This is the Think Tank. Welcome!" The lady at the desk, a prim but stressed-out assistant, was introduced as T. T, short for Teresita, had been with the company for more years than she cared to count. She'd landed a PR job right out of college and, at an event one evening, met Mr. Heidt, Jr. The next thing she knew, she'd quit PR and become his personal Executive Assistant, a job coveted by many. T oversaw everything, especially when Mr. Heidt was gone. Various doors leading to management offices surrounded her desk.

"Oh yeah... a *ton* of thinking goes on in here," someone loudly commented from inside one of the adjacent offices.

"That's Vivian, our PR Manager and local comedienne. Hi, Vivian! How's the PR world going?"

Vivian popped her head around the corner to greet Brandi and Mary.

"The world is about to come crashing down. Other than that, it's all good. Welcome, you must be Mary. Need any events? You should always fill out the sheets. They're kept up here." She pointed to an acrylic file holder on the wall. "Good luck. See you around."

In the meantime, the phone had been ringing off the hook. T finally peered down to look at the caller ID. "Oh Lord. Not her again. She's a real pain in the ass."

"Wait! It isn't Mrs. Clockstop, is it?" said Vivian's voice from behind the computer monitor.

"That's a real name?" whispered Mary to Brandi, who had already moved on mentally.

"No, thank God. That issue had to do with returning a fifteen-year-old worn and washed bra. It's been resolved. We had to give her a credit to her account! So stupid." T picked up the receiver.

"Executive Office. Good afternoon, how may I—" Rolling her eyes and shaking her head, a look of great anguish crossed T's face.

"Oh, I am very sorry that you had such a bad experience. I really am." She glanced over at the girls and grimaced, then continued. "We are all about providing you with the very best in customer service."

"Come on, let's go. This may take a while." Brandi mouthed the word "Goodbye," as they started to move out of the executive offices back into the store.

"Day in and day out, that's all she does, field calls from angry customers wanting an explanation as to why they've been treated so unfairly."

"And have they?" answered Mary innocently.

"God no! They're just sad, lonely and desperate, and have no one else to complain to."

They were now back on the sales floor.

"See that customer over there? The one with the giant platinum bouffant and the pink mink coat?"

"Yes," said Mary, while Brandi took another sip from her Yeti. "She is one of the wealthiest women in Texas, if not America. Last month she purchased a $14 million-dollar diamond necklace."

"Wow!"

"That should keep the company afloat awhile longer."

"What do you mean?"

"Well, I probably shouldn't say this, but... the HeidtMoore is in serious trouble."

"But that's impossible! This store is amazing. It looks to be doing very well, particularly if you have people like Mrs...." She gestured toward the mysterious woman.

"Dinkleheimer."

"People like Mrs. Dinkleheimer making large purchases."   "That's true. The real bread and butter for the company are the incredible personal appearances—which we refer to as 'PAs'—that the store has. Everything depends on the PA. We have one a season and it's a big deal." She gestured wildly with her hands before taking another sip.

"Really? What was your favorite personal appearance?"

"OMG! It has to be Michael Jackson and his chimpanzee. But we also had this designer…. What was his name?" She clicked her fingers, trying to remember. "Oh yes, Karl. As in *Lagerfeld*. It was held outside the store in a Texas horse arena."

"Wow, that's amazing. So who do you have coming this season?"

"We don't know yet. These types of events are *very* confidential. A lot is riding on this season's event and you could not have come on board at a better time. You'll definitely be involved. Whatever it is, it sure better be the best one yet."

"Why is this one so important?"

"You want to know the truth? I heard that we are actually $10 *billion* dollars in debt." Looking around to make sure nobody was near, Brandi quickly added, "but you didn't hear that from me."

Mary paused to wonder if that was one reason that Mr. Heidt was never around. It was hard to believe that a store with as much history as the HeidtMoore could actually be on the brink of closure.

Out of nowhere, Olga approached.

"Hi, Olga."

"You both conspiring. What? You look for deal. I have deal." Her arms were yet again loaded with expensive handbags.

"Olga, not now. This is Mary. She is our new Children's manager."

"I know. I know Mary. We met already. She want bag?" Olga was not one to give up on a sale. Like a spider casting her web and not letting go of her prey.

"No. She doesn't want a bag." She turned to Mary. "Wait. You don't, do you?" Mary shook her head no.

But it only took a second for Mary to second-guess whether she needed the bag or not, "Maybe I do… what is this?"

She felt the peacock-blue crocodile doctor's bag, unable to resist the temptation of touching the exotic piece before her. *Caught!* Olga smiled.

"Well, Mary, I will leave you and Olga. Enjoy! I hope that you've had a great tour. Call me if you need anything." And just like that, the tour was over and Brandi went back to her office, Yeti flask in hand. Olga didn't even notice her leave.

"Brand new. No one has. I sell this one. For you. YSL. All yours. Very nice. Now you will work very nice here and I sell you this bag. More expensive one is better one. You want?" Relentless in her pursuit of the sale, Mary was finding it difficult to walk away.

Making up an excuse, Mary finally left and tried to find her way out of the store, leaving Olga and her handbag. She was relieved to get away from the saleswoman and finally go home after such an exhausting day.

Mama's House

Mary was finally home an hour later. She flung herself onto the couch, exhausted and exhilarated from the day. She heard the sound of her mother's cane pounding on the floor.

"Here Mama," Mary called out.

Deloris limped into the living room.

"*¿Mi amor, que haces?* Where have you been? You said you'd be home two hours ago."

"I know, I know." She waved her mother off. "I got the whole tour of the store. It took longer than I thought."

"Next time you call me, ok? I'm so excited to hear what it is like, you must tell me everything." Mary knew that this was an exaggeration but at least her mother was trying to be positive for Mary's sake.

"Sorry I'm late. But Mom, it was amazing. The store is incredible. It took the entire day. They have the most magnificent aquarium. Like, Mom, it starts at the bottom and goes up through the second floor, the third floor and then all the way to the top. And then on another floor, guess what they have? They have this area that's like a grocery store, but better. It's like a market, kind of. And they have this huge chocolate fountain. You would love it."

"No, no *mi hija*. You know that I have diabetes. *¿Porqué?* You tempt me."

"Oh, Mama, relax. Relax. You should at least come in and see it."

"Ayee. I don't like you working there." Since Mary started at the HeidtMoore, she had been home late at least three times during her first week. Her mother worried if the job was going to be too much stress for Mary.

"Mama, we've talked about this a hundred times. It's fine."

"I saw the news the other day. Linda Langley, my favorite reporter, was talking about that fashion person, John Galileo. All those drug problems and racist comments."

"Mama! And what does Linda Langley know about fashion anyway?"

"She sees the person. Beyond the fashion. What Linda reports is truth." Seeing that Mary was visibly upset, Deloris decided to soften her tone. "I just want what is best for you. Retail. Fashion. It's aggressive. It's no place for a young girl like you to work. I just don't want you to think...."

"Mama, I'll be fine."

"Okay, well don't say that I didn't warn you! One day you're clucking along like a chicken in the yard. The next, you're the Sunday roast on the table of a rich man." Reflecting on her younger days, before the accident that left her with a limp, Deloris was not going to let Mary get caught up in a world of things, designer labels, and men who would break her heart. Deloris had only dated Mr. Heidt, Jr. for a while before she knew that their relationship was not what she wanted for the rest of her life. The long working hours, after-hour parties and packed social calendar were not things that kept a family together. Distracted by her daughter, Deloris stopped thinking about the past.

"Ah, Mama! Enough. Enough." Changing the subject and getting up from the couch, she walked toward the kitchen. "I'll have dinner ready in a few minutes."

Pushing her mother's negativity aside, Mary slept peacefully that night. She dreamed about all of the possibilities that the HeidtMoore had to offer, from her relationships with coworkers, interesting customers, the exciting personal appearance—*what responsibilities will I have?*—and of course Igno..., no Istafno..., no, —*no that's not it, his name just rolled off his tongue so smoothly*—Nacho. *Nachooo.*

Sloan's Connection

Sloan Garrett was the other Assistant General Manager of the HeidtMoore. He was strikingly different in comparison to Boggs Daniel, not only in appearance—where Boggs was tall and slender, Sloan was shorter and a little on the pudgy side—but also, in management style. Boggs's tendencies were to "go with the flow" and be a cheerleader for all. Sloan, on the other hand, was an exaggerated micromanager to the umpteenth degree. The only thing that these two had in common was their drive to be the next GM.

Sloan had gathered all of the supplies that he needed to work on the customer service bulletin board down by Loss Prevention—more commonly referred to as "LP"—taking with him glitter board, glue sticks, and scissors.

"T, I'll be downstairs if you need me." T acknowledged him with a nod and continued typing away at her computer.

Downstairs, in the employee entrance hallway, Sloan began to work, glue stick in hand. It seemed that the bulletin board was a passion of Sloan's. It was a way for him to express his creative side.

While he was busy gluing little smiley faces to the board, his phone rang. "Sloan here." It was T.

"Yes, you have an important call from your cousin Hayley."

"Can you take a message? I'm right in the middle of something important."

"I can, but she said to tell you that it was urgent."

"T, I'm covered in glue and happy faces." Nothing ever interrupted Sloan on his projects. At that moment, Mary was walking past him on her way to lunch, noticing the new board and glancing at Sloan with a smile.

"She wants to speak with you about a potential Hudson Hawn personal appearance." Sloan waved down Mary and mouthed, "Here, finish this. I have a call." He shoved the glue stick and supplies into Mary's hands, nearly losing his phone. *So much for a lunch break.* Mary didn't know

Sloan very well, but she knew enough from the month that she had been there that he was demanding and not particularly well liked by the other managers. But before Mary's father had passed away, he told her something that she would never forget, "Remember the silver rule, *mi hija*. Treat the unkind with kindness. Teach them." Being new to the store, Mary found herself repeating this mantra daily.

Sloan, without even a thank you, turned away, rushing down the hall, still on the phone not missing a beat.

"I will be right there." He hoped on the elevator. *What could Hayley have to do with Goldie Hawn and Kate Hudson?*

Hayley was a third cousin on his mother's side. Like Sloan, she was a distant relative of Mr. Moore, the very man who started the HeidtMoore back in the early 1950s. Sloan remembered the days growing up when he spent summers with his cousins at Heidt Ranch. Of course, the Heidt family members were always present as well. Mr. Moore and Mr. Heidt had grown up best friends, and they both had entrepreneurial spirits.

Sadly for Sloan, none of his ingenious ideas ever took off. Deep down, from a very early age, he knew that he would be in retail. It was in his genes. He had ten brothers and sisters, but he and Mr. Heidt, Jr. were the only ones still working at the HeidtMoore proper. He knew that if he could stay a few more years, when Mr. Heidt retired, the store would be his. Running the massive department store was his destiny. Fortunately, he also had a few other cousins working in the corporate offices who kept him looped in about any big changes that the Board of Directors was considering. This inside knowledge made him feel important. He also had a good relationship with Mr. Heidt, enough to feel in charge when the boss was not there.

The elevator reached the fifth floor and Sloan quickened his pace. He picked up the phone and dialed Corporate.

"Hayley Moore, please." There was a long wait until finally she got on the phone.

"Cousin! You are not going to believe who I have secured for your store!"

Hudson Hawn PA News

Decorated like someone's great-grandmother's living room, Sloan's office showed off his taste for chintz and florals. The terms "hip" and "cool" were not in his vocabulary. The most contemporary items were the recent thank you notes from customers pinned to the walls. Aside from a vase of fresh peonies on his desk, everything seemed dated.

"That is fantastic news! So, we are the only store? Yes, yes, we will be ready. We have four weeks. No, thank you. Okay, bye." If Sloan was going to rise to the top of his career at HeidtMoore, this personal appearance with none other than the great designers Kate Hudson and Goldie Hawn would clinch the deal. They were currently the hottest design team, splashed across every social media site and in all of the fashion magazines. True, it wasn't your traditional designer appearance like, say, Karl Lagerfeld, but they were celebrities and celebrities were hot right now. In order to pull this off, Sloan would need to convince the senior executive team and that might be tricky. He looked forward to breaking the news to Boggs, as it would be Sloan and not Boggs who would be responsible for putting on the biggest show of the spring season. This fashion show was everything.

♦

Later that morning, the team met in the conference room at the back of the executive offices. Sloan, with a smug smile on his face, had an announcement for those present: Brandi, Boggs, Vivian, T, and Pietro, the visual manager.

"I need your full attention. I have something very big to tell you."

"Shoot!" Boggs's catchphrases bugged the shit out of Sloan.

"I just received some very important news. We are going to have a fashion show. Not just any fashion show—" He stopped suddenly. "Wait, are you taking notes?" he asked pointedly, looking in the direction of

Vivian. She was not impressed with these impromptu meetings, which she could tell served only for Sloan and Boggs to outdo one another and were a waste of everyone else's time.

"I'm not writing anything because you haven't said anything!" Vivian said, defiantly standing her ground.

"I'm getting to it!"

"Alright, alright. So we have a fashion show."

"Yep, got that." Vivian was never one to miss a beat.   "I have booked Hudson Hawn!"

"What!?" Boggs was astonished.

"Hudson Hawn? As in, Goldie and Kate?" Pietro thought that this was actually a new low for the store.

Brandi was not entirely sure who or what anyone was talking about, but she picked up on Sloan's tone that this was really important. "Yaaay!" was all that she could say.

Sloan excitedly tapped the table and bounced up and down in his chair. "YES!!! Isn't that amazing? I can't believe it. This is huge. They have not done a fashion show at a department store ever! This is bigger than big."

Vivian reached into her giant Chloé handbag and brought out a yellow lined notepad and a pen.

"When are they coming?" Boggs was having a hard time concealing his jealousy that Sloan was going to be putting together a fashion show with one   of   Hollywood's   most   celebrated actress/designer/healthguru/mother-and-daughter teams.

"I'm getting to that. We have four weeks, people. Only four weeks to pull off this extravagant event. We wish we had more time but that's how it is. Very tight time frame. I need everyone on board. So... any ideas?"

"Whoa, whoa, whoa. Wait. Four weeks? For real?" Vivian was not happy.

"Yeah, we can do it." Sloan said optimistically.

"That is hardly any time. We need invitations, press releases, food and setup. Like, what's the idea? What are the elements to pull this together?"

"Let alone convincing our customers that this will be bigger and better than any other designer coming to the store." Pietro would have to work extra hard to conjure up an exciting visual for this event. He loathed Hollywood actresses.

"He brings up a good point. This isn't exactly Zac Posen."

"Boggs, we'll have lots of animation and people will love it. They will!"

"Is there going to be a bar?" Brandi was good at reinforcing positivity during their meetings. Sloan needed to get the ball rolling and convince the executive team of his idea: "Goldie loves extravagant. She sees flowers in winter, snow in the sand. She is fashion. She is life. After seeing her latest collection, I propose that we present a Cinderella-meets Russian hooker-meets—" Vivian was less than thrilled at where this was going.

"Sloan, did you just say… hooker?" Incredulous at the thought, Vivian couldn't take it anymore. Where was Mr. Heidt to enforce order when she needed him?

"—secret-garden theme and we can decorate the runway with gardenias!" Boggs was going to make sure his stamp was on the event no matter what.

"I kind of like that, Boggs. Not bad."

"Sloan, you kind of like that? Do you even know what our budget is!?" Vivian was about to walk out.

On the defense, Sloan suggested that the budget was still in the works but maybe several thousand dollars, which would cover everything from a pre-show cocktail party, marketing, models, setup, and the production of a fashion show with fifty looks.

"For that amount, we might even be able to afford a "wow" moment. What would the "wow" moment look like?" Vivian was definitely going to have to take the lead in this.

"Something sexy."

"Something *chic*. What about… um… we have kissing booths?" Boggs was a little off base, but still trying to capture the narrative of the celebrity designers.

"It's already been done. Sloan, any ideas?"

"Dancers. They could perform on either side of the stage and throughout the preshow party. Ballet dancers?"

"Too expensive. Unless we do high school kids and we are NOT doing that. Anyone else?"

"Hooters. I know people who work there." Not knowing whether or not Brandi was serious, they all agreed to pass on any dancing component altogether.

"Let's move on for now. Let's discuss the guest list."

The meeting ended up lasting an hour and only a few decisions were made. One was to have another meeting.

In Case of Emergency

The next morning, there was a manager meeting before the store opened. It was a pregame huddle, a time to get focused and make any important announcements. The biggest announcement, of course, was the fashion show. Sloan was bursting to break the news.

Mary, Starbucks in hand, stood beside Sarafina, the manager of Precious Jewelry, who stood next to Chef, who unknown to everyone other than Mary, had his hand on Brandi's bottom. Mary looked quizzically at Chef's large hand. Beside them was Nacho and a few other managers. It was the usual suspects. Sloan stepped into the center of the room to quiet the assembled group.

"Welcome everyone. This will be quick. I just want to tell you all about a very important event 'happening' in our store in a couple of weeks. Yes, the long-anticipated PA." Managers clapped upon hearing the news.

By the way he was bobbing up and down on the balls of his feet, Sloan was very excited. "But first, let's discuss yesterday's business."

Everyone moved uncomfortably in place. Chef removed his greasy hand off Brandi.

"I know that things weren't good for a few reasons. No one likes to shop when there isn't a promotion going on in the store and online has a free gift to offer. Then there were the server issues and not being able to reach clients because we can't get phone service. But guys! No excuse!" He raised his voice. "That is no excuse. We did 350 on a plan of 850. That is not acceptable! We missed our goal by half-a-million dollars." Frantically bouncing more, Sloan continued. "I mean guys, this is ridiculous! We have to make this up. Are your associates writing thank you notes to our customers? Are you telling them all that we can match online promotions? Okay. Now let's go around the room. I want to hear what is going on today in each of your departments."

"Okay everyone, we have a very important new security procedure—" Nacho spoke up first but was quickly cut off by Tevi, the manager of Handbags and Cosmetics.

"Wait. Before we begin, I want everyone to know that our Glamzone Glow reps, all of the way from NYC, are coming in today around lunchtime. So please invite your associates and customers to shop in Cosmetics. We must look really good. As you know, I'm new to that department since the last manager did not come back after her maternity leave."

"Yes, thank you, Tevi. That's enough. Now, Nacho."

T cut in first. "May I just say, along those lines, that everyone should know that Mr. Snorez will be here today for lunch." T always told the team when certain clients were coming in, so they had advance notice and could plan accordingly.

"Oh crap."

"Oh boy!"

A few other managers grumbled at the near mention of his name.

"He's special, really special. I'm gonna need to prepare his favorite turkey tortilla with braised short rib," Chef added. It took Chef longer to prepare Mr. Snorez's meals than those of any other customer.

"We have that on the menu?"

"No, Tevi. We don't."

"Okay, everyone, that is enough. We know that he is difficult, we just have to make his experience as exceptional as possible. Okay? Now, listen to Nacho please. This is crucial security information, particularly with our BIG event coming up." The room became silent.

Nacho cleared his throat and flexed a muscle, picking up a box filled with tiny, red nylon backpacks.

"Yes, thank you. I personally put together these bags myself. You cannot take security too lightly." Nacho began handing out a backpack to each manager.

"Thanks. What the hell is this?" Ignoring Tevi's question, Nacho continued down the line passing them out.

"Thanks."

"Each bag contains crucial elements, in case we are—"

"What? In case we are what?" Despite Tevi's tough exterior, she was sensitive and harbored a fear of the unknown.

Nacho needed to be strict but not cause any panic among the managers. "Should anything happen. That's all I'm saying. We can't be too careful."

"Thank you, Nacho. Very thoughtful." It was almost time for Sloan to announce the big designer duo.

Looking around the room, Mary could tell that these red bags weren't going over very well with the team.

Nacho opened one of the packs to show the managers what was inside. "See, right here you have your hydration." He pulled out an 8-ounce water bottle. "Then you have a power bar to keep you going, should you run out of food. Here," as he pulled out a small, bright yellow flashlight, "you have a flashlight, should we lose power. And finally," as he pulled out a laminated card, "you have a guide on what to do if we have an active shooter."

"Oh Lord." Tevi was not impressed with this ridiculousness.

"Sarafina, why don't you read out loud to the group what it says."

"Sure." She took a deep breath and started to read.

"'In case a person coming into the building happens to have a gun, walk up to them very calmly. Tell them in a reassuring tone that they are welcome to shop but must remove the gun from the premises.'
Seriously?"

"Keep reading."

"'Should the situation become aggressive, walk out to the nearest exit.' What if he shoots you? It doesn't give you much time to walk anywhere, let alone to an exit." All of the managers verbally agreed in unison.

"Well, obviously you won't just stand there. You'll do what you need to do. Isn't that right, Nacho? I mean, guys, come on. This is a guide to what to do. We all need to be aware of this."

"What if they come in and start wielding their gun and...."

The music had turned on in the store which meant the store was open and customers were coming through to shop. The managers started filing out.

"Great information, Nacho. Also, very thoughtful. So, did you make the bag yourself? Very resourceful! Okay, everyone. That is our security update. Have an opulent day!"

Mary was one of the last to leave the office along with Nacho. He was walking through, carrying the remainder of his emergency packs to a few of the managers left behind.

A funny feeling came over Mary. She just wanted to give him a big hug.

"That was really great."

"Really? No one seemed to care." He seemed so downtrodden.

"Not true! We just aren't used to someone taking the time, that's all. You really are concerned with our safety. That's wonderful."

"Thanks. You're sweet," replied Nacho as he walked on ahead of her.

Mary couldn't help but stare. He was so handsome. Suddenly, out of nowhere again, Olga appeared with several boxes of shoes and a few handbags draped around her neck. "Mary, Mary, these are last ones.

Your size."

How does she know my shoe size? "Hi, Olga. No thank you. I have to get back to my department."

"I bring bag to you. It last. Last one. I make you deal."

Wanting to escape quickly and hoping that she would forget, Mary replied, "Fine. Bring it by and I will take a look."

Sloan and His Dog

Another successful day. Thankfully, sales were up, a drastic contrast to the prior day. To celebrate, Sloan opened a bottle of vintage Jordan Alexander cabernet and thought about what to cook for dinner. He didn't have to cook for anyone. It was just he and Peanut, his giant golden retriever puppy. Pouring himself an exceedingly full glass, Sloan remembered that he never actually mentioned who would be coming for a personal appearance. *Shit!* Not to worry. He would just have to hold another meeting tomorrow. With that decided, he texted every manager with the subject line "MANDATORY MEETING."

All Sloan wanted to do was sit and watch TV for a bit and relax. All Peanut wanted to do was play. He kept leaping up on Sloan's lap with a tennis ball in his mouth.

"Okay, okay. I know, you want to play. Let's go." As he got up from his couch, he opened the sliding door to go out to the garden.

It was a beautiful cool spring evening. Just Sloan and his dog. The truth was he longed to have someone to share his home with him. It was time. He couldn't remember when he last had a date. The last serious relationship he had was twenty years ago, when he had ventured out to Miami to live and work at a Restoration Hardware store. He'd shared an apartment with a guy who later decided that he would prefer to be with women. Since then, a part of Sloan had just given up. What was the point? But now, maybe he should try. What could it hurt? He was tired of being alone. That's why he got Peanut, but Peanut could only provide so much comfort. Nope. Sloan was a lonely middle-aged man who was starting to get a little potbelly. His only companion was a dog.

While the dog played, chasing his ball around the yard, Sloan took out his phone and typed in the Google search bar: "BEST GAY DATING APPS FOR SINGLE MEN."

Mary Quite Contrary

It had been an exhausting day in the Children's department. Mary had a few coaching sessions with her staff on the importance of presentation standards. *How hard was it to line up hangers two inches apart on a bar, sized small to large, so that the hangers facing you looked like a question mark?* She was bewildered by how this was such a difficult task for some.

In addition to monitoring the staff and working through some customer issues, Mary had found time to sneak down to the Fine Apparel department. She had been eying a Dolce & Gabbana sheath dress since starting her job at the store. She finally had earned enough in commissions to purchase it with her discount.

Her afternoon was spent in a committee meeting that she had just learned was required in order to participate in HeidtMoore Accounts. A team of managers from around the store met once a quarter to discuss ways to get their sales associates on board with opening credit card accounts for their customers. In an age of credit cards and rewards programs, this seemed like an easy task. But it wasn't. Therefore, a committee was formed.

After the meeting and a few hours in the department, Mary headed home for the day.

◆

"Mama, I'm home. Samson, have you had dinner?" Mary yelled as she walked into the house. Samson thumped down the stairs, bouncing his basketball.

"What's in the bag?"

"Oh. Nothing. Where is Mama?"

"She is outside watering her plants. I'm starving, what's for dinner?"

Mary headed to the kitchen, dropping her handbag and the

HeidtMoore garment bag on the couch. Deloris came in through the back door, a watering can in one hand and her cane in the other.

"*Mi amor*, how was your day?"

"Good. Busy. Oh, you won't believe what happened!"

Samson chimed in, "What happened? You broke a nail?"

"Worse! Every toilet in the building stopped working. Can you believe it? In a store as huge as the HeidtMoore—with restrooms on every level, including the disgusting employee one in the basement—there was not a single one that worked for nearly two hours."

"That is unbelievable. You see, why do you want to work there? Looks can be deceiving. The building looks so beautiful on the outside, but inside it sounds like it's falling apart."

"I know. It is so strange," Mary replied, as they sat down to eat at the dinner table.

Deloris could see the couch from her seat and proceeded to ask Mary about the garment bag.

"What?" Mary said defensively. Mary wasn't interested in sharing the details of her purchases but couldn't help feeling the slight pangs of guilt for being distant toward her mother.

"You purchased *another* outfit? This is your third purchase this month. How much was this one?"

"Mama. Stop!"

It was too late; her mother had already discovered the price tag. "$2,500? What were you thinking?"

"It's nothing. We get a 55% store discount. It's nothing."

Her mother continued eating in silence.

Another Day, Another Meeting

Another morning meeting happened. The Dress Collections manager, Hilz, spoke first. "Since I couldn't come in yesterday, may I make an announcement?

"Sure. But please keep it brief." Sloan needed to keep this meeting on track.

"I have exciting news! We just received a new shipment of Kylie Jenner dresses and they look amazing. I doubt the pieces will last a week. Please tell your associates to come by and take a look today."

"Thank you, Hilz. It's an important line for us, guys. Sarafina, what's happening in your world?"

"There's the pre-personal appearance luncheon in a month. Mr. and Mrs. Gottrocks are hosting the event. To launch the new, 'Yours and Mine' diamond line, in conjunction with whomever we get for the PA."

"Nice. Tevi?"

"Yes. I have three new handbags. 'I Have and You Don't.'"

"Well. That's obvious. You just brought them in."

"That is the name. They are completely unique because the client picks their own lining, and each is personalized with this hang tag." Tevi held up a four-inch LED tag that read, "I Have and You Don't."

"Wait, what is the name?" Boggs said, walking through the door. Sloan rolled his eyes and groaned in annoyance, knowing that now Boggs had arrived, he would never be able to finish the meeting on time.

"'I Have and You Don't'." Tevi repeated.

"Oh, our customers will love that."

Sloan needed to keep moving and make sure Boggs didn't disrupt the flow of the meeting. "Great, thank you for bringing the 'You Have' bags, Tevi. Anyone else?"

The room was silent. Just what Sloan was wanting, having everyone's attention. "Okay!!! So, we have a—"

"Sorry, I have one." Brandi quickly spoke up, remembering that she needed to discuss the trainings. "In a few weeks, we begin our annual trainings. Bloodborne Pathogens, OSHA, and Credit. It's important that we are at 100% completion. Get your associates started right away. Ok?"

"Thank you, Brandi. Now we have—"

Chef now cut off Sloan, moving slightly toward the center of the room to address the managers. "I didn't mention," he said, his hand a little too close to Brandi, "that we have a lobster bisque special and are running a Kobe beef burger just for today, folks."

"How much?" Tevi always liked to discuss food.

"Err, cheap. It's leftovers from the weekend, so with the employee discount, we're talking twenty bucks?"

"Not bad. Cheaper at Del Franco's Chop House though. Just sayin'."

"I beg to differ."

"Let's not argue about the price of Kobe. Okay? Thank you. Now as I was saying, we have a very, very, very special event. The personal appearance you've all been waiting for. In just over a month, we have none other than... drum roll...."

Everyone started tapping whatever they had handy to make the desired drum effect.

"Hudson Hawn!" The drumming abruptly stopped. A few managers clapped, but it certainly wasn't the applause that Sloan wanted. Maybe they were distracted by the talk of Kobe beef? Or simply wanted to get out to the floor and do what good retail managers do best: manage and sell?

"Isn't that exciting? Yeah! I know you all can get at least 100 customers each from your departments to attend the fashion show."

Sarafina spoke up first. "What in the world? How am I meant to sell the Gottrocks on the celebs turned... 'designers'? I don't mean to be snobby but—"

"Well, you are." Sloan was not pleased with her attitude.

Sarafina was worried and she had good reason to be. If her luncheon, a prelude to the personal appearance, was a failure, she could risk taking a $3 million-dollar hit with major ramifications for the company.

"I thought we'd at least get Tom Ford. Bloody hell, I'd take one of the Kardashians at this point!" Tevi protested.

"Are you sure? Hudson Hawn?" said Hilz. "This is amazing, OMG!"

"Okay for you. Precious Jewelry sells in a day what your department sells in a year." Tevi never shied away from the facts. But her tone could always undermine any manager, associate, or executive.

Sloan needed damage control. Fast.

"Think of it this way. They are coming in and bringing their famous friends. Hello? George and Amal? Hello? Tom Cruise? I mean Hudson Hawn is gaining momentum in the world of fashion and we are on the forefront. Big article in *Women's Wear Daily* just the other day about the power of their influence. Guys, this is big." No one responded.

Giving up, Sloan concluded the meeting. "Okay, make it an opulent day everyone! Sarafina, may I see you in my office, please?"

All of the managers left, leaving Sarafina to follow Sloan back to his office. As she entered, she had a sinking feeling in her stomach.

Sloan motioned to Sarafina to take a seat.

"Everything set for this afternoon? Are people responding to the 'Get A Genie' promo? I'm thinking that would drive your luncheon."

"Yes, sir. I'm just hoping all of the RSVPs show up. You know how it is."

"I certainly do. They say that they're coming, then just don't show. I don't get it, I really don't. At least you know the most important person won't let you down."

"Mrs. Gottrocks?"

"She is wonderful."

"Yes. She is." *God. Where was this going*? The conversation was not what she had anticipated. Sloan continued.

"So, since this opportunity came up this morning, I need you to sell the Gottrocks on Hudson Hawn."

"But—"

Sloan raised his finger to stop her from interrupting. "I know that you are skeptical but there's no need. This is an exciting opportunity. And you know that they know everyone, so what we need from them is at least an additional 50 people. What do you think?" Sloan had the strangest way of charming anyone who might disagree with him. Sarafina was giving in to him and she hated it.

"But you know she only wears custom Armani."

"Don't worry about that. Hudson Hawn has some similar things. Go on, see what you can do. I'll put some swag aside for you. And maybe a little extra incentive." Sloan raised one eyebrow and rubbed his hands together. Sarafina finally agreed to ask her client. Then she got up and left his office. *Why did there always have to be another agenda?*

Promos

The birds were chirping. The air was crisp. The bathrooms had been repaired and the servers were up. Mary had become familiar with the eccentric manner in which the store ran. It would be a wonderful season ahead. She just knew it! Despite the stress of having to achieve incredibly unrealistic sales numbers on a regular basis—and in particular for the personal appearance—it was spring, and a very good time to start at the HeidtMoore.

Almost three months had passed since Mary was hired and she had acclimated herself to the HeidtMoore very well, learning everything that she could. She still had not met the real Mr. Heidt, which at times felt strange. He was always out of town, or sick, or his car didn't work. Or there was the time his handyman had supposedly fallen through his roof, so he couldn't come to work that day. Odd, but maybe this was how things were in every retail environment. The giant department store seemed to run itself. There was so much going on in the store and so much to understand about how retail sales worked, particularly when it came to the barrage of promotions.

Today was going to be the day that she would learn all about the promotions and incentives that the HeidtMoore had to offer their special customers. It would also be a brainstorming session to enhance the promotional opportunities for the Hudson Hawn PA. Mary was looking forward to the class. Not only would she be honing her skills in the art of selling, but she would also have an additional opportunity to earn more money. She calculated just how many sales of Le Colt designer oven mitts she would need to pay off her mother's mortgage. At $500 a pop, she could sell five a month to reach her goal. And that was only a children's item. *Imagine selling a handbag or a couture gown.*

By the time Mary was asked to attend the training, she felt very comfortable in her role as manager of Children's. She was pretty much used to the spoiled kids destroying every visual display in sight. She was used to the snobby moms ordering the nannies around and treating her as if she were the maid. She was even used to late-night "homies" who frequented the Burberry shop every weekend and the pick-up lines that they used to get her attention. The one thing that kept Mary up at night was worrying about the promotions. It was astronomical how many there were to drive sales. Worse still were the goals set by Boggs and Sloan. The "promos," as they were called, all had names such as "The Most Wanted List," "Squared Out," "The Real Deal," and "Art of Friction," each one designed to entice the customer. With these promos came presell.

The term "presell" had a curious history and Mary found the concept absolutely fascinating. Before the days of "promos" at the HeidtMoore, associates would sell all kinds of luxurious products to any customer who walked through the door. Easy. Done. Customers liked what they were getting, and the sales managers made their sales goals. Then, like a deadly disease rippling through the retail world and beyond, the financial crash of 2008 happened.

Along with other brick-and-mortar stores, the HeidtMoore needed to readjust how it was doing business. And so, it was decided that there would be many more lucrative promotions instead of only two large sales a year (one being in the summer and the other in the winter). Marketing and public relations teams were brought on board to figure out creative ways to lure customers. Then the sales staff started being assigned sales goals that they would have to reach. Year after year, the goal got higher and higher. Corporate marketing teams could determine whether or not the promotional events were working, and whether or not the company was making any profit. To reach the assigned goals, associates would "save" sales, waiting to ring up the transaction until the promotion began. Over time, this holding became known as presell. But now presell had become one of the biggest headaches for associates because customers were savvy. They didn't have to wait anymore, now that online was doing the same promotions and offering the same incentives.

◆

Mary entered the freezing cold training room where the class was being held. She wished that she had brought a sweater instead of her new cotton Marc Jacobs dress. *The room was colder than a meat locker.*

Surveying the training room, Mary saw a few familiar faces, including Olga and Tevi, and she spotted Zane, the man whom she'd met on the first day in Cosmetics, with his slick black coif. But Mary didn't recognize the tall woman standing in front of the class in a starched white blouse and with her bleached blond hair in a tight chignon. She was Barbie, the class instructor, and beside her was a stocky man with wire spectacles, small eyes and a double chin. He didn't say much and he looked like an accountant. Just as Mary got to her seat, Barbie started the class.

"Now, we all know why we're here, don't we?" It was Barbie's patronizing tone that made Mary second- guess why she was in the room. Was she in the right class? This seemed more like detention than a class for eager hopefuls like Mary.

Barbie continued, "I am here with my colleague. Say hi, Bryan." The man beside her sheepishly took his hand out of his pocket and did a little wave. He had very small hands.

"If you did not do well with the 'Get a Genie' promotion that just ended last week, then that is why you are in this class."

What? Mary hadn't done that badly, had she? Most of her team had done well. All of the confidence that she'd felt earlier escaped her now.

"Or," Barbie continued, "if you have not taken this class before."

Relieved to be part of the second group, Mary relaxed. More than anything, she wanted to succeed and to do well, especially with the big personal appearance coming up. She believed, until this point, that she was well on her way. She may not have understood all of the reasons behind the promotions, but she did understand numbers. She loved numbers, and selling was just a numbers game to her.

At the back of the room, across from Mary, sat an older, more mature woman.

"I haven't a clue why I'm here," the old woman croaked, revealing signs of years of smoking in her voice. Mary smiled at her sitting there indignantly. Mary guessed the woman must've been somewhere between the age of 80 and 90.

"Ethel. Do you suppose that your sales at the bridal boutique have anything to do with it?" said Zane, addressing the older woman.   "Do with what, exactly?" said Ethel, with defiance in her voice. Mary went bright red. Was this woman being defensive or simply hard of hearing?

Barbie interjected, "It seems that you have underachieved in the last three promotions and I am here to help you learn some tricks and new ways to reach your selling potential." Barbie was somewhat of a dictator. "We have a very important personal appearance coming up and you must reach your sales goal."

"I still don't understand a word she's saying." Ethel said to no one in particular.

"Get your pens out. Do you have a pen? If you don't, Bryan will give you a very special pen. Pass the pens, Bryan," she said, as she nudged him toward the class. "We are going to write down the top five reasons why people love shopping at the HeidtMoore. Then, on the back of the paper,

I want you to write down why they might not like shopping at the HeidtMoore."

Mary leaned over toward Olga, "Do you still have my pen?"

"Pen? Me? No."

"I gave you my pen when we met, and I forgot to get it back."

"Me don't have any pens."

Finding that difficult to believe, Mary tried once again, "It's special. My mom gave it to me."

"No. I never see it."

"But I swear I gave it to you. It's a gold pen. Remember? You were trying to sell me the bag when I was going to HR. You put it in your purse, I think."

"Ah, pen? Your gold pen?"

"Yes, that's the one!" She was relieved to be getting somewhere.

"No. Never see it."

Mary gave up pursuing. It was the principle of the matter more than anything. Olga had blatantly stolen the pen and it simply wasn't right.

Once Bryan had unwittingly opened his box of cheap Bic pens, with the logo, "Give Moore. Get Moore. Reach new Heidts!" Olga grabbed the first pen distributed from the box. Despite having a purse load of pens at all times, she always found room for another. Never missing anything, Tevi leaned in to Mary.

"Hey, you. New girl. Word of warning. Olga is a fraud. She steals everything. Pens, rulers."

"It's true." Zane chimed in.

Olga's reputation for taking any pen in the store was renowned, evidenced by Mary on her first day. Olga didn't care. She was probably selling them to the Russians back home.

"Are you writing? Let's begin. As you continue to write, I want you to think about events like the upcoming 'Art of Friction.' Why is it so important? What can your customers gain? Can anyone tell me? Olga? Why don't you take a stab."

Olga nodded in agreement. "It is chance to sell customer best merchandise for cheap."

"We don't like to use the word 'cheap,' Olga."

"Oh. Next to free."

Dismissing Olga altogether, Barbie looked around the room. "Who else?"

No one had anything else to say.

Next up was Barbie's teaching tool, a PowerPoint presentation. It contained a lot of clip art. On the screen were the words, "Gift a Genie," with clip art gold lamps covering half of the slide. Barbie talked endlessly about the benefits of the Genie (some gimmick to increase the sales margin), how it was created (by a mid-level marketing intern), who benefitted (no one) and the impact (giving more people who can't afford to shop at the HeidtMoore a reason to come in).

Mary gazed across the room to see if anyone else was any less interested than she was. Olga was staring into space. *What was she so deeply thinking about? Pens?* Then there was Tevi, the manager of Handbags and Cosmetics, whom Mary met during her first week. She was chatting in a loud whisper at the back of the room to another lady. Mary kept hearing "bloody this" and "bloody that" in her thick Indian accent. In the short time that Mary had been at the store, she noticed that Tevi was always complaining. Mary looked back at Ethel again, sitting beside Olga. It was as if Barbie was reading Mary's mind.

"Ethel, what is the benefit to the customer for the 'Genie' promo?" Ethel smiled. Barbie then repeated a little louder, "Ethel, the benefit?"

Ethel finally replied, "What? The benefit? Yes, you tell us about the benefits. I just love them." Ethel had not heard a word of the training.

Barbie decided on a short break. "Take a break. Please be back in your seats in ten minutes. We have a lot more to cover, plus... a fun game."

Tevi rolled her eyes. Everyone gathered their belongings and left the room. When the class resumed, only about half of the attendees had returned. Olga, Tevi and Zane were nowhere to be seen. Mary took a seat next to Ethel.

After hours of grade school games and several more PowerPoint presentations, Mary left the class feeling more confused than when she entered that day.

Sparkle

"Oh my God! Like, pull it together!!!" said Tevi, watching over her associate Sparkle, who was on the verge of tears. It was another day and another berating by Tevi. Sparkle was a delicate associate who continued to get demoted year after year. In Sparkle's first year, she sold nearly $800,000, much to the surprise of her superiors and jealous colleagues. That was her first year of glory and since then it had been a downhill slope. *Sparkle had better get her act together. She is a complete liability.* Tevi was desperate to get Sparkle's performance up to standard. Aside from a wealthy client who later became a nun, most of Sparkle's clients were wild, eccentric and penniless. It was beyond reason why any of the executive team—Mr. Heidt, Boggs or Sloan—would think that Sparkle would be a good fit.

A shy, thin girl with straggly red hair almost reaching her waist, Sparkle had to be handled as gently as the kid gloves which she sold at the HeidtMoore. Most of her time was spent off the floor, crying in a stockroom. Anything would send her off in tears. Poor Sparkle. She meant well—very well—and was always eager to please anyone and everyone. She was a girl afraid of her own shadow.

Boggs bounded through the department, knocking over Sparkle's carefully wrapped and folded gloves.

"Well, there goes the last two hours of work," Tevi said under her breath. Upon hearing this, Sparkle started crying again, stopping Boggs in his tracks.

"Hey, hey, hey... what's all this? C'mon, don't cry! Here, let me help you." Boggs squatted down and picked up the gloves strewn all over the floor.

"Mr. Boggs. That's very kind of you. I'm fine." She didn't notice the customers coming over to see what was on the floor.

Sparkle repeated her self-help mantra.

"I'm fine. Really!"

"No, you're not."

"I am. Really."

"You're crying."

"Oh, it's nothing." She said, as tears streamed down her face. Smeared black lines of crusted mascara streaked her flushed cheeks.

The store was busy. Customers, tourists, children, grandparents... everyone was coming into the glamorous store for something. Suddenly, Boggs and Sparkle were surrounded by people, who began picking up gloves and walking away with them, as though it was some sort of garage sale.

"I'll take these," said a woman who used her walking cane to pick up a pair of kid gloves with mink trim. On the other side of Boggs, several Japanese tourists, cameras around their necks, stood haggling over prices.

One said, "This free?"

Boggs immediately jumped in. "No, nothing is free! These fell from the display." Paying no attention to Boggs, the man walked away with the merchandise. "Hey, wait, where are you going?"

It was too late; these random strangers were putting the gloves on and walking away.

Boggs jumped to his feet and called after a Japanese tourist with a fluorescent-pink Hello Kitty backpack. "Wait! You can't do that! They are for sale!"

Spinning around, he saw another person take multiple pairs with him, nodding his head in agreement with Boggs. "Sale! Ahhh. Very good!"

Tevi approached the mess and sniffed.

"Where's my bloody inventory?"

"Bandits took everything," Boggs said, looking at the remaining two mismatched gloves lying on the floor.

Tevi fixed her gaze on Sparkle, "This is all your bloody fault."

"But I didn't do anything." Sparkle was helpless. She hoped Boggs would come to her defense, rescue her from this situation. But he did little to defend her.

"Yep, your manager has a point. We better call LP."

Sparkle panicked.

"But?"

Boggs took his phone out his pocket and dialed.

◆

Nacho had just sat down to eat his low-calorie, gluten-free, zero-fat, sugar-free smoothie, part of his fitness regime, when the phone rang. He was looking forward to his meal. Until Boggs called him.

"Boggs here. Nacho, we have a situation. Several customers are walking away with gloves. Nahhh, not paid for."

"Can you describe what they looked like?" Nacho was always on duty.

"One was Asian, possibly Japanese. A girl. There was a man too, possibly Japanese."

"Okay... what were they wearing?"

"Blue denim. Actually, it may have been a dark blue dress on one and a baseball cap on one of the guys."

"There was more than one guy?"

"There were a few. There was also another woman. With a cane. None of them were together. See what you can do about getting the gloves back."

"Sure, I'll review tape."

"Think we've got time for that? These guys move pretty fast. Look at the screens to see where they are. One had a Hello Kitty backpack. You need to find them now. Before they get away. They took everything."

"You just said one had a cane." With seriousness in his voice, Nacho inquired further.

"It's probably a fake cane."

"There are a lot of people in the store with canes. It's going to be hard to track down these people."

"Go after the lot of them."

Nacho put down the phone and shook his head in disbelief. Then he walked over to the store monitors to see what was happening. Surely, if it was serious, Brad, who was eating a bag of popcorn and staring at the screen, and Danny would have told him.

"Guys, check Handbags and Accessories. We have a situation."

◆

Meanwhile, Boggs's work was done. He said goodbye to Tevi and to Sparkle, who hadn't stopped crying, and walked on to the Shoe department.

Cookie Monster

Mary sat in her office, finishing up her tracking sheet for the Hudson Hawn personal appearance. Each day, Sloan requested that the managers provide the number of confirmed RSVPs as well as the dollar amount for any preorders. To say that it was stressful was an understatement. Sloan called at least five times a day demanding to know how much effort each manager was putting into the event. Mary was exhausted. There she sat, at her desk, going over the numbers and figuring out how much more she would need to make her goals.

She heard the clinking of a cookie jar. Jars of cookies were kept in every manager's office so that they could give them out to customers. It was all part of a customer service initiative. However, more often than not, the managers would consume more than the clients.

Mary glanced at her snack drawer. *No.* Lately it had become a tendency to stress eat, particularly when she didn't meet her goals. Looking at the giant calendar above her computer she was reminded that it was one month until summer. *Tempting.* She heard the clinking again. Was there a mouse? There was a rumor that the HeidtMoore had a rat problem. Mary chose not to believe it. But now she was curious what was going on. She scooted her squeaky chair over to the door. She had always been lame at eavesdropping.

She heard whispering.

"Those cookies are for customers. You can't eat those!"

"What? Oh."

The sound of cookie packets being tossed on the counter and the scampering feet made Mary came out of her office. No one was there and the cookie jar was half empty. It made her skin crawl when things were out of place. Everyone on her team knew that everything had a place. From merchandise standards to office supplies, she had her team trained.

Mary raced down the hall, getting closer to the perpetrators. *Who was this cookie monster?* As she ran down the hallway she wondered if it was Rebecca, one of the sales associates in Precious Jewelry. She was not one to miss a meal. But would Rebecca really hike up two floors for a lame cookie? She could barely move from one counter to another. *Who else could it be? Sparkle? It must be.* When Mary started at the HeidtMoore, she and Sparkle had bonded quickly over doughnuts one morning. Sparkle had had a disastrous date and Mary had found her crying in the handbag stockroom. Of course, it was by accident. Mary had been wandering through stockrooms trying to get familiar with the layout of the HeidtMoore. Her self-guided tour was delayed as she ended up listening to Sparkle spill her guts about some guy who sounded like a loser.

Mary reached the end of the hallway. She could hear voices coming from a stockroom. She peered inside, where there were six OST team members doing markdowns.

"Hi, were any of you in the Children's stockroom just now?"

Silence.

Then the sound of pricing guns. *Beep. Click. Beep. Click.*

"Ok then, I am going to LP to check the cameras, no big deal." Mary turned to leave the stockroom.

"Wait. It was me." Mary turned back around. It was Ben, a shy Filipino who was new to the country and who had only recently started at the HeidtMoore.

"Did you just throw a pile of cookies on the counter?"

"Yes, but I didn't eat them."

"I realize that, but why didn't you just put them back in the canister? Why mess up someone's area?"

"I don't know."

"Well, just remember it's always best to leave places better than how they were. Respect your work areas." Mary left.

Beep. Click. Beep. Click.

♦

A week later, Mary found herself sitting in the executive offices, waiting for Brandi, who had called her up for a meeting. T was having an animated conversation on the phone. It turned out to be with the head of Operations. Mary wondered if it had anything to do with her team. Tempting as it was to eavesdrop, Mary thought better of it. Brandi walked by the glass pane of the door and motioned for Mary to follow her. As she opened the door to go into Brandi's office, she was overwhelmed by a strong scent. It was a familiar and potent smell. *It was definitely tequila.* Mary had heard the rumors about Brandi and her drinking problem, but in the five months working with her, this was the first time that she really thought they actually could be true.

"Mary, we have a little issue. And by little, I mean liii... ttt... le. Tiny. I can't even believe that we have to have this conversation," she said, laughing a little. "Someone has had their feelings hurt." Dramatically, she made crying actions with her face and hands. *Was this appropriate behavior for an HR manager? No, but it was a little fun to watch.* Brandi continued, "Ben came to my office the other day and was in tears over some cookie incident. Mary, please tell me he wasn't crying over spilled milk." She was laughing hysterically.

"Well, not exactly. It was really just a lesson in respect." She filled Brandi in on the story. "I addressed it as a group because a group of them was involved."

"Well you did right thing." Brandi was still laughing. "Ben needs to grow a pair of—oh, I probably can't say that, but it's true—big balls. I do have to let his boss, Willy, know."

This conversation was just awkward on so many levels.

"I understand. If you need me to sit in on the conversation, just let me know."

But Brandi shooed her off as she picked up the phone, so Mary got up from her chair and left to go back to Children's.

T's Story

It was morning in the executive offices, and T was already in deep with customer issues. The store had only been open an hour. Another angry customer. One after another.

"Yes, yes, I do understand. That is why I am trying to help you resolve the issue." T was already feeling overwhelmed as she tried to resolve the issues and maintain the ever-growing RSVP list for the Hudson Hawn PA.

"You know nothing," spat the customer at the other end of the phone, causing T to hold the receiver away from her ear. "Let me tell you." He continued.

T waited to hear what information Mr. Knox would share with her next. Silence. "Well, are you there?!"

"Yes, I am here, Mr. Knox"

"Don't patronize me!!! Do you know how much I spent last year? I spent $50,000. One year alone. Probably more than you will ever make in a lifetime. So why don't you tell me why, if I am such a great customer, I haven't received my gift card yet?!"

The truth was Mr. Knox was not a "known" customer. His spend in the store was a mere drop in the bucket compared to top customers. It didn't matter; great service was great service, and it was T's responsibly to make sure every customer was treated equally. Typically, T could handle any situation that came across her desk, making distraught customers feel loved and confirming that their accounts were in order. Unfortunately, Mr. Knox was not going to be appeased or, obviously, planning on going away anytime soon. T placed him on speaker phone while he continued his rant, and walked to the kitchenette in the back of the office to make herself a cappuccino from the Keurig.

♦

Later that afternoon, the executive offices were quiet. Except for the sound of the fluorescent lights above T's head and the occasional tapping of the keyboard, all was calm and peaceful. These moments were sacred to T. She was normally besieged with customer complaints, constant phone ringing, new promotions to review and communicate to the store, and other miscellaneous store projects. In short, she kept the place running.

"Hey gorgeous."

Great. Peace shattered. T knew that it was too good to last and if anyone was going to shatter T's happiness at this very moment, it may as well be the creepiest of all creeps: Willy, the head of Operations.

She pretended not to notice his comment. But, as was his custom, he just stood there in front of her desk, staring. He was licking his lips like a giant toad about to catch a fly. *Disgusting.* All as she sat at her computer pretending to type.

Finally, T said sharply, "What is it, Willy?" Every time she met him, it became increasingly more difficult to hide her revulsion of this man, his demeanor and his eyes looking her up and down.

"Hey," with pretend hurt in his voice, "Don't be like that. Why are you being so mean to me?"

T would not fall for this tactic. She could see right through him. She wondered if it had ever crossed his mind that she could easily report him to HR for his continuing sexualized behavior toward her. Of course, she would never do that on the chance that it could be turned against her and misconstrued as racism. Willy may use the fact that as an African-American man, he was being profiled. Who knows? This couldn't be furthest from the truth, but T wasn't going to risk it.

As his bulky frame stood closer to her desk, dressed in an ill-fitting grey OST uniform, she stopped banging away at her keyboard. She looked up at him.

"Let me ask you something."

He moved a little closer. "Oh, Now you talk to me. I'm all ears, sweets." He gave T a sly grin and arched one eye brow.

"Okay. First, don't call me sweets. Second, are you married?" Willy's eyes widened, and T could see him practically salivating. She felt nauseous. He put his large, chapped and blistered hand on T's monitor.

"Don't move closer. Answer the question."

"Ouch... ouch. You're feisty."

But before he could answer, Boggs jumped into the room like an excited puppy.

"Hey, T. Check the list, we gotta hot sale 'bout to go down. Oh yeahhh." He turned to Willy and give him a fist bump, "What's up, bro!?"

Why did Boggs always act like he was one of the brothers? He was as white as white men can be. For once, T was actually pleased at the distraction.

Then Mary and Brandi entered.

"Willy, good. You're here. Mary and I need to have a word with you."

"Okay, okay. Sure. Now? Okay. Let's go. I'm ready. You know me. Always ready."

Boggs was checking the promotional RSVP list on T's desk and Mary could tell that Willy was noticeably on edge.

"We can talk here. It's only T. You don't mind, do you?" Brandi looked at T with a sweet smile. T knew she meant well and didn't take it personally, but still simply resented being made to feel like a potted plant. The truth was that after T's second divorce, she felt worthless. Her dreams of becoming a soap opera star had crumbled years ago and now her life was nothing but dealing with overprivileged customers, fighting off perverts and checking a shitty promotional Hudson Hawn RSVP list to see if a shitty, rich HeidtMoore customer was on the damn thing. Not that she was stressed-out or anything.

"Brandi, have I done anything?" Willy stuttered.

Except for stare at my boobs for the last ten minutes? T remained quiet.

"We have an issue with one of your team."

"Oh Lord. Which one?"

"Mary caught Ben acting inappropriately."

"Oh my. Oh my, oh my...." Willy was in disbelief.

"He apparently had his hand in the cookie jar."

"Ah, jeez. He did?"

T looked from her computer, sat back in her chair, with a look of satisfaction on her face. Finally, the rat would be caught.

"Yes, Willy, he did. It's not good." The gravity of the situation suddenly weighed heavily on Brandi. She was not happy.

"I'm sure there's been some misunderstanding."

"No, Willy. Apparently not."

"He tried to steal my cookies!" exclaimed Mary.

"I'll handle this, Mary. Thank you." Brandi whispered to Mary.

"Nooo. Oh my. I. Do. Not. Believe. It. Will we press charges? What will happen?"

"There will be some sort of action."

"I swear, I swear I did not teach him. I swear. Are you okay, Mary? Brandi, could I have a word privately?" As they left the room, Mary decided to browse the list.

"May as well, since I'm here."

T was astonished by how well Mary was responding.

"Are you okay? You're handling this really well."

"I mean, what am I supposed to do? It's only a bag of stupid cookies but it's the principle."

"You mean cookies. As in, the things you eat?"

"Yeah?"

Meanwhile, Brandi and Willy were huddled in the conference room at the back of the executive offices. Willy was perspiring, wringing his hands and speaking in hushed tones.

"Mary went to see you and wants to press charges?" He couldn't believe what was happening.

"Actually, he approached me."

"You too? Wow. He's got balls."

"Willy!"

"Sorry! I'm in shock. Sorry, sorry."

"Will you have a word with Ben and make sure he stops this behavior? We want to make sure he doesn't do this to anyone else in the store or there will be consequences. Got it?"

"Got it. Yes, ma'am."

Brandi left the room and Willy followed shortly thereafter, passing T as he headed toward the door of the executive offices. T tried to capture his attention.

"So, back to my question Willy."

"I gotta go." Willy didn't stop or even look in her direction. His demeanor had certainly changed.

Boggs was always oblivious to the nuances of situations.

"T. This Hudson Hawn event is going to be awesome. How much do we have in presell? The event's gotta do 2.5. What've we got?" Glancing down at a sheet of paper with scribbled numbers, T read from her notes.

"It looks like Children's has 5 in."

"On a plan of what?"

"Er, 8?"

"That's not good. That's a shitload of baby crap. Ha! Get it?"

"No."

"Never mind. It looks like Mer is dealing with a cookie issue. She'll be fine. Okay. Who else?"

"Dress department has in 4."

"Good!"

"On a plan of 15."

"Ohhh. Fuck. T, read me the good stuff, come on. There must be a few departments that are gonna get us to our goal. Give me the heavy hitters." *Boom.* Slamming his fist on the table to emphasize his point,

Boggs knocked over a jar of pens. "What about the Cosmetics department?" T solemnly shook her head from side to side.

"You don't want to know," she said, kneeling down to pick up the pens.

"Call down to Cosmetics and tell everyone there that for every 8-ounce jar of La Mer, they can get $100."

"We have that in the budget?"

"I don't know! Make up something. Anything!" *Boggs was going into panic mode.*

"Okay."

"We don't make this event, we're screwed. Done for. Say goodbye to having a personal appearance. May as well kiss goodbye to our jobs."

"I wouldn't mind." T was a little hopeful.

"What else?" Boggs said, choosing to ignore her comment.

"Ok. Good news. Handbags has in 12 on a plan of 16."

"Now we're talking."

The phone started ringing again. T sighed, picking up the receiver. "Executive Office. This is T."

Boggs took the paper and scanned it to see if there was any other department aside from Handbags that was going to save his job. Meanwhile, T had another issue to resolve.

"Nooo. She wants to return the bag? But why?! You're sure? Hold on," cupping the receiver, she turned to Boggs.

"Boggs, need your help."

"What's wrong?"

"It's Olga. Her client, Mrs. Heffer, wants to return the custom Balenciaga."

"What? No, she can't do that. That's a $50,000 return. Not today. Nooo! Is it within the 60-day return policy?"

"It's not within the return policy. It was purchased two seasons ago.

"No. Simple. Absolutely not. No. We are not taking back the return. Ridiculous."

"I'll let Olga know." T loved saying no to associates. They always felt like they took advantage of the system. "So, I talked to Boggs and there's no way. We can't do it. I understand... yes... I understand... okay... no, we're not taking it back, particularly since she used it and there are stains... no... I'm sorry... I understand—"

"Give me the phone." Impatient with how the conversation was going, Boggs motioned T to hand over the phone. She reluctantly handed it over to him.

"Please, not the bag. She can't return the bag. Not today of all days!? Oh... oh, I'm sorry Mrs. Heffer, I didn't realize that it was you. Nope, not a problem at all. I'm happy to return it. I'll be right down. Thank you. Not a problem. Of course, we'll take the return." He put the phone down, defeated.

"But you said we weren't taking back the return?"

"I didn't exactly say that."

"Yes, you did. I don't believe it."

"It's better to please the customer. That is what we stand for and sometimes you have to make the exceptions."

"But... we made an exception for this customer before."

"T. Don't argue with me. I am going down to the floor to handle the return."

"This is a shitty day. What about our presell?"

"Don't swear!"

T was speechless and now she was being told not to swear. It was at that moment that a small Filipino man popped his head around the corner.

"Hello. You T?"

"Yes. How can I help you?" She was taken by surprise by the intrusion.

"You have cookie?"

"I beg your pardon?"

"My name Ben. Cookies for client. Need bag." His English was terrible, and T wondered how long he had been in the States. She also wondered why he needed cookies for his client. He worked in Operations as a picker. He didn't have any clients. *What the heck.*

"Sure. They are around the corner in a small brown box. Knock yourself out." At this point, it didn't matter. *If we could take back an expensive handbag we may as well just give away everything.* He bowed to her... three times. T didn't know why but she found it very irritating. He took a handful of cookies and walked backwards, bowing as he went out the door. He was an odd bird.

The Gottrocks Luncheon

The Handbag department, adjacent to Precious Jewelry, was looking especially opulent the morning of the much anticipated pre-Hudson Hawn luncheon hosted by the Gottrocks. They had agreed to host this event and were generally pleased to be part of the Hollywood duo's big debut.

Sparkle had wanted to call out sick that morning due to overwhelming nausea but she needed the money badly, so she forced herself out of bed, off the toilet and into the store.

She was checking her phone and absentmindedly sorting through designer handbag price tags when Tevi walked up with a large cart of boxes.

"Sparkle, we have to move these damn handbags. If not, Corporate will yank them. Please re-merchandize the front case and get all of the 'I Have and You Don't' bags out."

"Yes, ma'am. I will get right to that. Right now," said Sparkle quietly. Tevi didn't believe her.

"Are you sick?" She looked at Sparkle's blotchy eyes and red face.

"No, I'm not sick."

"Are you crying?"

"No. I'm fine. How many bags would you like me to put out?"

"There are about fifteen styles. Maybe twenty. They are all over there on that cart." Sparkle was staring at her phone, not paying any attention. "You better not be upset about some guy."

Putting down her phone and trying to stay focused, Sparkle said, "I'm going to get these out."

"Good. Get a move on. Then you need to get prepared for the day. With the luncheon, we can expect a lot of business." Tevi was depending on Sparkle to make her sales goal. As Tevi was leaving, she dropped a box of doughnuts on the cart.

"Here. Have one. You need it."

I can't believe I slept with him. What am I going to do the next time I see him? Pushing the cart of handbags over to the case line. Sparkle started unloading the "I Have and You Don't" handbags.

♦

Stuck in her own world, Sparkle failed to notice Rebecca, the overweight Precious Jewels sales associate, waving at her from across the aisle trying to get her attention. She wanted the doughnuts. Rebecca was in her late forties, with flaming red hair and fiery personality to match. She was one of five women who worked in the Precious Jewelry department, otherwise known as "PJ." These women were known around the store as "cougars" and the department was their lair. They were ferocious and would go after anything and anyone, especially the young rich men who walked through the store. It was one of the most important departments in the HeidtMoore, accounting for $200 million dollars worth of business a year.

Beside Rebecca sat another equally large woman. Her name was Liz.

"This is Liz speaking. Oh! I was just thinking about you... uh huh," said Liz while putting on her reading glasses. "Yes, yes, I'm working on Thursday." She flipped through her appointment book, each of the huge sparkling rings on her pudgy cougar fingers catching the light. "When does your flight arrive? Uh huh, okay. Will you have your driver or should I arrange to have a car bring you to the store? Yes, the necklace is one of a kind and the diamonds are some of the best I've ever seen. They will be perfect for the personal appearance. Yes, I know, Goldie has one *just* like it. Looking forward to seeing you... yes, you too... kiss, kiss...."

"Who was that? Mrs. Metmash? We need her to come in today. If we don't match LY to TY, we will face a major decrease for STD," said Sarafina, approaching Liz's counter. She always spoke in cryptic sales jargon, most of which no one completely understood. The reality was that, when referring to LY and TY, she could have simply said "last year" and "this year." As for STD, it stood for "season to date," not "sexually transmitted disease." Although due to the behavior of some associates, one could never be sure.

"Uh huh," said Liz, picking up a copy of *Town & Country*. She never listened to her manager.

At the end of the jewelry case line was another woman, leaning against the counter and smiling seductively at a young man looking at a series of diamond rings. This was Ally. Ally was an ex-model who had been married five times and was always looking for the next catch.

Toward the back of the department stood Susan, a seemingly sweet lady in her late sixties. Her looks were deceiving. This woman was as fierce as the best of them.

"I just got my lips done. I like them. What do you think? You don't you think it is too much, do you?" Rebecca always needed reassurance from her colleagues and was rarely provided with the truth.

"Nooo," Liz responded, without an ounce of truth.

♦

It was time for Sarafina to lead the pack into the event room, near the back of the department. This exclusive room was decorated exquisitely with crystal chandeliers and Herend china. Van Cleef & Arpels window boxes lined the room, each filled with estate jewelry and rare, one-of-a-kind baubles.

Like a pack of animals, the PJ associates all rose and sauntered into the room.

From across the sales floor, the Loss Prevention team was keeping an eye on the store and, in particular, on Precious Jewels.

"Wow…. Look at them go."

"I don't believe you, Brad. Stop staring, get your mouth up off the floor and get your job done. We got a department to take care of." Nacho had one goal: to become Corporate Director of Security for the department store and corporate offices. In order to do this, he had to enforce order day after day.

♦

"Mr. Gottrocks and his wife will be here at any moment. The place looks beautiful." Sarafina was thrilled with how the space looked.

"Too bad we didn't use the Baccarat instead of the Waterford. Oh well…," said Liz, moving aside one of the place settings.

"Listen everyone. We must anniversary LY for their anniversary this year. If it doesn't happen, I will have to see the GM about TY and try to explain not hitting LY."

Rebecca, finishing off a doughnut, was interested in knowing how they would make the day. "But how are we going to hit $3 million? Like, how many more diamonds can one man have? I'm just sayin'."

"A lot. Make it happen." Sarafina was already exasperated and the luncheon hadn't even begun.

"Yah. Easy for you to say."

"Rebecca, please."

"Do you need help?" Liz asked Rebecca.

Oh dear. No. Not now. This was exactly what Sarafina's feared: her associates getting into a catfight right before the luncheon.

"I don't need help. I just... I don't know. It's such a commitment. Yah know? Like, hello? Oh, I have $3 mil to spend today."

"Dear Sarafina. if our colleague here cannot do it, I assure you, I can." *The claws were out....*

"Bitch."

"Ladies! Please! Now, let's have a good day and do our best. Ok? Everyone on board? TY is only 4% more than LY so I think that we can, in my personal opinion, achieve this."

Ally whispered to Susan, "Oh, those two. Rebecca is such a slob, how she sells anything is beyond me." Keeping her opinions to herself, Susan decided not to comment.

◆

As guests started arriving, Sparkle looked like she had seen a ghost. Behind the renowned Mr. Gottrocks was a very handsome young man.

"That's the sort of man you need. Not the sort of fuckups you've been with," Zane said, mysteriously appearing in the Handbag department from the Cosmetics floor. Unlike Sparkle, he always spoke his mind. Sparkle said nothing.

"He's so handsome," said Zane in a dreamy daze.

Tevi appeared, interrupting their conversation. "Sparkle! Go get the gold 'I Have and You Don't' bag from the back. You have to make a special delivery. Go. *Now.*"

"The Gottrocks want the bag? You never told me that?"

"Yes. They want it. Don't argue with me. Go!"

Sparkle scampered back to the stockroom to find the bag for her manager.

Thoughts were racing through Sparkle's mind. *Will he remember me? Why hasn't he called? Who is he here with? Wait, is he married? Maybe that's why he hasn't called. No, he isn't married. No ring, I remember. Did I tell him I work here? Or did?*

Five minutes later, Sparkle returned with the merchandise. Zane noticed that Sparkle was distressed. "Are you ok?"

Tevi, not even noticing Sparkle's shaky hands, forced her to go with her across the aisle to the luncheon.

They were met by Security at the door.

"Where are you going? You know that it's a private luncheon. Only the PJ associates and their guests are allowed," Brad said, reviewing his list.

"Yes, you don't think I don't bloody know that. I have this bag for one of the guests. Sparkle's taking it in." Tevi pushed Sparkle toward the door.

"Well, I was never told about this bag. Her name is not on this list. I can't let her in."

"Brad, this is ridiculous. Let her in. Go on, Sparkle. Go in."

Before Brad could say or do anything, Tevi and Sparkle pushed through the door.

The doors opened to a long table where the guests were seated. Obviously, it was an intimate affair. Sparkle spotted Mr. Wonderful near the end of the table right away. Tevi turned away for moment to talk to Sarafina and failed to notice Sparkle dash over to the end of the table where the Gottrocks' grandson was sitting.

"How does Sparkle know Mr. Gottrocks grandson?" a perplexed Sarafina asked Tevi.

"What? She doesn't. Don't be foolish," Tevi retorted, as if it was the worst thing she had ever heard.

"Apparently she does. Look over there." Sarafina pointed toward the end of the table where Sparkle appeared to be pleading with the handsome young man.

"There's more to that girl than meets the eye," said Liz, who wasn't often wrong.

Tevi stood in surprise with her mouth wide open. "Shit! Fuck! Bloody hell!"

◆

It was blatantly obvious that Mr. Wonderful was trying to ignore Sparkle. But after several attempts he could not conceal that a sales associate was begging for his attention. "Yes, how can I help you? Have we met?"

"Hey, it's me. Remember? In Uptown at the Dram. The night of dancing?" Sparkle hoped that she did not sound too desperate.

"No, sorry. I think that you have the wrong person." Mr. Wonderful was embarrassed as he looked around to see that everyone had stopped their conversations.

"What you mean? It's me. Remember? I loved our night together so much. It was amazing. I just... I have to talk you. Can we go somewhere?"

"I don't know this woman. I don't know what she's talking about," Mr. Wonderful said, addressing the guests at the table. Sparkle started to tear up.

Mr. Gottrocks summoned security and within moments Nacho was pulling Sparkle away from the conversation.

"But wait. Wait! No. You must remember! Stop! Let go of me!"

"Okay, Sparkle. Calm down. No need to raise your voice. Let's go." Nacho was talking to her like a baby, soothingly trying to calm her down. Turning to the guests, he said, "It's all right everyone, please continue. We are leaving now."

As Sparkle was dragged out, her face was filled with desperation. "Stop! Please let go of me!" Like a mental patient being taken to an asylum, Sparkle was carried off and the luncheon resumed in peace.

◆

Sarafina surveyed the room, "My God! I don't believe Sparkle was fucking a Gottrocks!"

Once the commotion had died down, Mr. Wonderful declared to the group of assembled dear friends and relatives that he would be making a substantial purchase: an 18-carat gold-and-diamond Patek Philippe watch once owned by Paul Newman. It was valued at more than $5 million.

Mrs. Dinkleheimer

One afternoon, during yet another promotion to drive the Hudson Hawn PA—this time, one called "Tick Tock Gift Card Time"—Mary was walking toward the executive offices through the Fine Apparel floor. Each dazzling gown was shining under the rose-colored spotlights, which accentuated the fine details of the clothes displayed. She imagined what it would be like to have an unlimited budget to be able to buy these stunning gowns. *It must be nice.*

As Mary tried hard to not be distracted by the opulence before her, she was knocked hard from behind.

"Ouch!" Mary let out a small yelp but managed to regain her footing. Before her was a woman, face down on the floor.

"My goodness! Are you alright?"

The woman slowly came to her feet.

"Mrs. Dinkleheimer! Are you ok? I am so sorry!" Even though it was Mary who had been hit hard, she still apologized.

"Oh, honey. I'm alright. I tripped over these damn new shoes, which my ridiculous sales girl sold me for the Hudson Hawn event. I knew they were bad when I got them. I don't even like wedges. Why I had her sell me these, God only knows. Do you think Kate wears things like this? I don't think so."

"I'm so sorry!" There she was again, apologizing for something that had nothing to do with her. "Here, let's take a seat over there. You did take quite a tumble." Mary guided Mrs. Dinkleheimer over to a plush velvet chair nearby, the sort typically reserved for the husbands or boyfriends or sugar daddies who waited while their wives, girlfriends or lovers spent hours trying on gowns.

Mrs. Dinkleheimer looked up at Mary. "You work here, honey?"

"Yes, I do. Actually, I've been here for—"

"Good. You can help me."

"Er? I mean, of course."

"You will get me a new pair of shoes that I can wear to the event and return these. I would just love that."

"Um... yes, yes. Of course. I will just need your size. Shoe size."

"You're sweet. They have all that in the system. I'll wait here."

"But... well."

"What is it?"

"What sort of shoes would you like?" She could not believe her luck.

"Whatever you decide. And charge it to my account."

"Okay. I'll be right back." Mary looked around for assistance. Not finding anyone, she proceeded down the escalator to the Shoe department.

On the second floor, as Mary exited the winding escalator, Nacho was standing there with his muscular arms folded. *God he was sexy.* She couldn't stand it that she thought this way. In his deep, manly voice, he acknowledged her and gave her a smile.

"Surviving your first couple of months?"

Flushed, she replied, "Oh, yes, you know. It's good!"

"Glad to hear it. You are a breath of fresh air around here."

Mary was completely flustered and finding it very hard to focus. "I have a quick, um, question. Do you know Mrs. Dinkleheimer?"

"Do I know? Seriously? Of course, I do. Why? Is she here in PJ again?"

"PJ?"

"Precious Jewels. She practically lives there."

"She wants me to find her a pair of shoes."

"In PJ?"

"No. She's in Gowns right now. I need to get to the Shoe area. I kind of forgot where it is again."

"What's she doing there? And what are you doing helping her?"

"It's a long story. I don't want to keep her waiting. Please help me. Please. I feel out of my element."

"Sure, I'll help you. You got it. And yes, you definitely do *not* want to keep her waiting. Follow me."

Nacho, like her own personal armed guard, took her by the arm and they made it through the crowds of people. They entered the Shoe department, which was designed like a library except that, instead of books, there was shelf after shelf of gorgeous shoes. Mary had never seen anything so decadent. The shoe cases were movable, and each case was sorted by color, height and style. It was incredible. Just a library.

"Met the 'Shoebrarian' yet?

"No, I don't think so. But this is incredible! How am I going to pick a pair for her from this collection!? Where do I start?"

"I'm guessing her associate is helping, right?

"No. I don't know who that is."

"Good luck. Listen, I gotta go. Emergency in Cosmetics."

"You can't leave me here!" Mary was panicked by the thought of navigating the library alone. Nacho turned back.

"Here's my card. Work number and personal cell, which I carry with me just in case. Should you need anything, just call me. Okay?"

Taking the card, Mary was relieved that she had someone whom she could depend on. Their hands brushed ever so slightly, and Mary felt a warm and tingling sensation. Then he disappeared into the store.

It was time to conquer the world of shoes, as quickly as possible, and return to her new customer. This was going to be a feat akin to climbing Mount Everest. With quiet determination, Mary charged forward.

◆

Mary was back with Mrs. Dinkleheimer, boxes piled high, within fifteen minutes. She couldn't be too sure and certainly didn't want to make a bad impression, so she brought many more shoes than was actually required.

"You are a dream! How clever you are to think of this," Mrs. Dinkleheimer said, pulling out a black Manolo Blahnik pump. Mary decided that it was best to start simple and head in the direction of flashy, if that was what this customer ultimately wanted.

"I will need something a bit more... I don't know... something with a bit more... oomph."

"Oomph? What about these?" Mary pulled out a pair of leopard Christian Louboutin flats, the red soles so polished that Mary could almost see her face reflected back in them.

"Adore! But no. I can't have leopard. It reminds me of darling Lionel. I gave him that name, after my father."

"Who's Lionel?"

"Lionel was the leopard who lived here at the store. He was in one of the window displays. I gave him to the store."

"Really?"

"He died last year."

"So sorry for your loss."

"He was a great leopard. May he rest in peace."

Mary decided that it would be best to change the subject... and the shoes. "Why don't we go with this pair?" Mary pulled out chocolate leather Jimmy Choo Mary Janes.

"Oh... now we're talking!" Mrs. Dinkleheimer said, taking the pair out of the white box and discarding the tissue paper.

Mary smiled, relieved that she was about to accomplish what she thought would be an impossible task. "Why don't we go down together to see the other shoes. Maybe there is another pair just for you?"

The VIP

From the far corner of the sales floor, Tevi was in a simmering rage.

"That bloody girl!" Standing behind the Chloé handbag case line was Sparkle. "I'm sorry!" she said, beginning to cry. "Should I show you the scarf collection another time?"

"No!" Tevi snapped back. "Those fucking scarves... just start laying them out." Then she spotted Mary walking through the department. "Ugh. Look at her."

"Who?"

"The new bloody girl. Mary. She is a nightmare. This place is shit. Absolute shit. How did she get that old money bags? That should have been my bloody customer. Unbelievable. I'll tell you, she is not to be trusted. You understand?" Tevi wagged her finger in Sparkle's blotchy face.

"I think that she's nice," Sparkle sheepishly commented.

"Nice? Nice! Are you crazy?" Sparkle opened her mouth to defend her new friend, but Tevi continued. "Don't answer that. It was a hypothetical question."

"I just—"

A customer approached the case line.

"I said 'don't'!" She turned toward the customer who had appeared at the counter. Hiding all contempt, Tevi graciously smiled. "How may I assist you, sir?"

"Hi. My name is Bob. You helped me four months ago."

"Ah yes. Yes, of course. I remember." Tevi was racking her brain, trying to recall who this man was in front of her. Bob wore a plaid shirt that Tevi guessed probably came from Macy's, and his jeans made him look like he worked on a construction site. He was also slightly overweight. *God, where did these bloody people come from?*

"You helped me with a handbag for my wife. If I got it, you were going to put us on the VIP list for Hudson Hawn. I'm not on the list. The

Executive Office doesn't have my name. Why? Why would they not have my name and where the hell is my gift card!? You do remember me, right?" said Bob incredulously. *He's married? How can someone like him be married? Life wasn't fair.*

"Let me make a call and see what we can do. Bob, what is your last name?" She started to scroll the contacts in her phone.

"If you remember me, why the fuck would you need to know my last name?"

"I, um, I have a lot of different customers." She was slightly put off and taken aback by how rude he was. "It will make it easier, that's all."

Bob, last name unknown, started to fidget, making Tevi wonder if it wouldn't be easier to simply go into the stockroom and call Customer Service or LP for help. There must be a way to find out more about this "Bob." He was being very uncooperative, so it was probably wise to get backup help, but not before giving it one last try. Besides, the VIP list was exclusively for top clients and Hollywood celebrities. There was no way that "Bob" would be in a room with Goldie and Kate drinking champagne and sharing stories. *No way.*

"Sir. I am trying to gather as much information as possible. What is your wife's name?" She quickly added, "Again?"

Then it was full-on meltdown.

"What the fuck do you mean??? What is her name??? You dirty hooker whore!!! You fuckin' salespeople are all the same. I had better be on the fuckin' list... or else!"

"Sir, please." She felt the situation getting out of hand. As if her day wasn't already bad, this crazed customer was making it worse.

"DON'T FUCKIN' MOVE!" He shouted the last two words while he reached into his pocket and pulled out a Glock, then pointed the gun at her. Tevi, panicked, turned to look for Sparkle for reinforcement. She was nowhere to be seen. *Unbelievable.*

"I said *DON'T FUCKIN' MOVE*, you Saudi Indian!" Then, he quickly swung the gun around at shocked associates and customers, some of whom were crouching down, some screaming, and others running for their lives.

♦

Mary, seeing the action unfold, quickly ducked down with her client, instinctively covering her with her whole body. Hiding behind a shoe rack, Mary peered out at the action from between two shelves of Louboutins. *Who was this lunatic? A crazed member of the Mafia? ISIS?*

Oh my God... was this really happening? Mary said a quiet Hail Mary and turned to comfort Mrs. Dinkleheimer.

"Don't you worry about me. I think that this is very exciting."

Mary was taken back by Mrs. Dinkleheimer's fearlessness. Suddenly, Mary thought about her mother. If this was it, if this crazed man with the badly fitting jeans planned on taking everyone out, who would look after her mother and her idiotic brother? They couldn't take care of themselves. It was always down to Mary to do this and that and to make everything right. She should never have been so insistent on getting this job. Her mother had warned her but never in a million years could they imagine anything like this.

In the corner of her eye, she could see Brandi staggering ever so slightly. *Was she injured or drunk? Where was Nacho?* She saw him arriving up the escalator. Like a Greek god appearing from the stormy clouds, he appeared to save the day.

"Stay there, motherfucker!" Bob was aggressive.

Nacho didn't seem to be phased one bit. "It's okay. Put the gun down. Everyone is fine."

"Who says? She hasn't put me on the fuckin' list. My wife *HAS* to meet with Goldie! And I want my damn gift card. You know why?"

"No. Maybe you would like to tell me? But first, put the gun down."

"I'll put the fuckin' gun down when *I* fuckin' want to. Got it? She ain't put me on the fuckin' list because she's a fucked-up Indian. All I did was come here to get one fuckin' thing and then leave. But oh no. I can't do that because this fuckin' Indian ain't got my fuckin' name on that fuckin' list. And I'm fuckin' pissed."

"I understand," Nacho said calmly.

Mary was enamored of Nacho and his bravery. Nacho was just the sort of man Mary longed to be with. If they got out alive, she imagined all of the stories that they would have. The memories that they would create. *If they got out alive.*

"So, what you gonna do? Punch me? I have a fuckin' explosive and I ain't afraid to use it." This was a man on a mission.

Nacho glanced over at Tevi, "Can we put him on the list please?"

"We don't—" Tevi quickly changed her tone. "Of course we can. I'm sure Goldie will be delighted at her special guest." Tevi was telling the biggest lie of her life.

"Are you fuckin' mockin' me? What a bitch. And for that you're gonna fuckin' get it," Bob said, raising the gun toward her.

Blackout

Suddenly the store went pitch-black. Total darkness. There could not be a worse time for a blackout. Unfortunately, the store had had three blackouts in the past month, what with all of the faulty wiring and the lack of a proper repairman.

Everything was complete confusion and chaos! Screams rang out. Gunshots were fired. Then, the heavy stomping of feet running away, disappearing into the store.

My God. What was going on?

"Get that bastard! He won't scare us!" Mrs. Dinkleheimer yelled.

"Mrs. Dinkleheimer, please. Shhh."

"I'm not scared of that jackass." Mary was shocked to hear that language from a woman like Mrs. Dinkleheimer. Her thoughts immediately went to Nacho. *Where was he?*

They couldn't see anything now. It was just black. Mary reached into her pocket to see if she had any matches or a lighter. *Of course not. Why would she?* There was a madman on the loose, and there she was, lying on her stomach next to the store's best customer.

◆

On another floor, Boggs had been merchandising new epicurean delicacies when the blackout happened. Even though he managed over half of the entire store, it was the Gift Galleries department that he felt needed the most work. The instant that the lights went out, Boggs made sure that his sales team was close, just like a Boy Scout. "We have a problem. No light," he said, pointing out the obvious. "Do y'all have your emergency packs?" He knew how to take control and calm down the associates, a few tenured women who presided over the area.

Betty, the coordinator who oversaw the area, stuttered, "Yes. Good... I... idea... Bog, I, er, Mr. Boggs. Where is the em... emergency packet?"

"Bett, focus! That's what I'm asking you. Now where is it? It contains a flashlight."

Betty stood there with her mouth open and a vacant expression on her face. Boggs had worked hard to train her to be a good manager, and she wanted to be a good manager, but she was flustered and muddled all of the time. It was an impossible task. This was no time for Boggs to wonder about Betty and her professional advancement though. He needed a flashlight. And he needed to lead his flock to safety.

"One last time, Betty... where is the bag that Nacho handed out to every manager at the last manager meeting? He handed those out in case we have an emergency. Like a blackout, which we have now."

"Or an active shooter," chimed in Lulu, a seventy-five-year-old sales associate with a hunch back and orthopedic shoes.

"An act... act... active shoot...?" Betty was so in shock that she couldn't spit out the rest of the sentence.

"Now Lulu, that will never happen. We're talking about a blackout. Nothing to panic about. Probably an electrical surge or something."

"Or the company hasn't paid its bills." A few other octogenarian associates croaked out small verbal agreements.

"Here it is. It was by my desk," said Lulu,

"Great job, Lulu." Boggs pulled out the small flashlight from the red nylon drawstring bag. Then he noticed the power bar and the bottle of water and pulled those out too.

"What are we meant to do with those things? Hit a gunman over the head with an 8-ounce water bottle?"

No sooner had she said that and Boggs had finished off the power bar and guzzled down the water.

"I guess there goes that idea...." Lulu's sarcastic candor was unnerving Betty, who was practically clinging to Boggs. Feeling replenished, it was time for Boggs to lead the group outside.

"Everyone follow me." The small glow of the light led them beyond the candy aisle and down past Fine China.

♦

The loud roar of a lion could be heard coming from the third floor. Mary heard its echo. *Where the hell did that come from?* This was strange as all of the exotic animals were locked up in cages in the basement. But there was a blackout in the store and an armed madman on the loose.

"Mrs. Dinkleheimer, are you ok? I think that we should head this way. I'm sure that the exit is this way."

"Exit? You think we're leaving? Honey, you've got another thing coming. We're gonna get that bastard."

"We are?"

"You bet your sweet bippy! I grew up on the prairies of West Texas and hell, you never knew what sorta trouble there was gonna be. 'Course those were in the days before oil, when we had nothin' but a pistol and a horsewhip to keep us protected. Bein' a woman, I learnt pretty darn quickly how to defend myself."

Mary was amazed by this remarkable woman. "Okay. Let's go get him!" Mary said, getting a bit ahead of herself. "How?"

"Don't you worry. I'll handle that part. Let's move."

And off they went, leaving the shoe library and into the dark hallways of the store. Mary could barely make out the shadows of the moving bodies, lumbering about in the dark. It was creepy. Mary barely knew her way around the Children's department, let alone the whole store. She wondered how they would make their escape. Then....

ROAR.

♦

Tevi was getting more and more irritated. "Come on! You can't just stay here. We have to go. A killer is on the loose."

Sparkle was wrapped up in a ball, crying her eyes out and refusing to leave the glass accessories case line.

"And don't sit on the Fendi scarf! You'll ruin it, and this is the only one left in the company." Tevi's last comment made Sparkle cry even more.

"I don't want to die!" Sparkle said in despair.

"You won't die but you can't stay here. Come on, we have to get out of here." Seeing that Sparkle wasn't about to move, she dragged her by the knees and pulled her out of the case, breaking a nail in the process.

"Jesus, Sparkle. Seriously?" Tevi almost collapsed with exhaustion, having pulled her associate, still in the fetal position, out of the bay. At least the tears had stopped.

ROAR. The sound of the wild.

"What was that? Was that a ringtone on your phone?" *Just the sort of nonsense that Sparkle would have on her phone.*

"No. I'm scared. That sounded like the lion."

"Don't be silly. It's impossible for anything to escape. You know what? You worry too much."

Sparkle began crying. Again.

♦

Boggs and his group came down the stairs of the fire escape. It was quiet. Too quiet. Boggs was perspiring. The air conditioning wasn't working, and he was responsible for bringing his associates to safety. He figured that the back stairs would be the best option since he could keep them huddled together, one by one. He hadn't accounted for the fact that several of them had undergone hip replacements and had difficulty walking, which was slowing them down.

A loud groan was heard. Then another.

It couldn't be... it was! Boggs flashed his light toward the sound, revealing two people moving vigorously up and down against the wall.

"My God!" Boggs couldn't believe what he was seeing.

Startled, the pair looked toward the light. Gasps came from the old associates. Lulu, being the ever-observant one, commented, "Oh! I've never seen one that big before!"

Betty stammered, "I... I... I... is that Chef?"

Boggs couldn't believe it. "Chef?!"

Chef and his mystery woman, who curiously looked like Brandi, picked up the remains of their clothing and scurried off into the shadows.

"Oh my... my... gosh. Boggs? What are you going to... to do?"

"Bett, forget you ever saw that, alright? Let's keep moving."

"I'm sorry we didn't see more." LuLu was never at a loss for words. "Who was the lucky girl?"

"It looked like the HR manager to me."

There was a collective gasp. "Nooo!"

Trying to gain control of his increasingly motley crew, Boggs turned to them. "Now listen, we need to focus. We need to get out of here safe and sound. This isn't the time for gossip, who's banging whom and where. No, we need to focus on the objective which is—"

"To get laid too," Lulu whispered to her compadre.

"Lulu! Guys, come on. Keep it together. I know that you're excited. It's been one rollercoaster of a day. I know it's a blackout and thanks to Nacho we have this flashlight so we can get back to normal and get back to what we're good at. Y'all hear me? Okay... now here's what we're gonna do. We're gonna go through these doors at the end of the stairwell and get outside. We can do this, team. You got this. Okay, can I have a 'one, two, three, GO TEAM!'" Everyone followed his cheer. Boggs always had a way of turning anything into a pep rally.

One by one, they slowly descended the stairs. But the door wasn't there.

Boggs surely had not missed the exit?

In the excitement of everything, he had led them to the basement.

"Guys. We gotta go back up."

"Lulu ain't moving," said Lulu.

"Then we have no choice but to go through the... animal cage. Stay close. We're going to have to go through the basement door, as it's the only exit down here."

They huddled together and pressed on, opening the door.

They entered. Sounds of birds flapping about, piglets grunting, and other unknown howls and snorts echoed throughout the narrow hall.

They carried on with only their small flashlight marking the way. Reaching the end, Boggs opened the door to the outside world. Daylight flooded their eyes. To their relief, they saw the resident zookeeper taming the lion and Nacho standing over a man in handcuffs.

"Active shooter is in lockdown." Nacho reassured the associates coming out of the store.

"Hey, I was right. There was an active shooter! A crazy lunatic in our store. Good thing Boggs was around to help our department," said Lulu.

Everyone was safe, the lion was caught, and the active shooter was heading to prison for a very long time. Just a typical day in retail.

♦

Nacho made a final sweep of the parking lot as the commotion died down. He spotted an older woman and young boy getting out of their car. They were slowly walking toward the front door.

"Hi, ma'am. I'm sorry, but the store is closed for the day."

"But the store is open until 8:00pm. It's only 7:00pm. Why is it closed?"

"Well, we had an unforeseen incident this afternoon."

"What do you mean? What happened?"

"Come on Mama, let's just go." Samson pleaded with his mother.

"Be quiet Samson. Sir, you must tell me what happened. My daughter works in there."

"Don't worry, everything is under control. No one was hurt."

"Hurt?!"

♦

In the distance Mary saw her mother and brother. They were talking to Nacho.

She called out "Mama, Mama" as she ran over to them. "Mama, you will not believe my day!"

"Wait! Slow down! Are you okay? Are you hurt?" Deloris was more concerned than ever.

"Ma'am, don't worry. There were no casualties and even the animals came out unharmed."

"What are you talking about? Mary, let's go. You are never coming back here."

"Everything is fine. Nacho is the one who caught the guy. He had a gun and the lights went out everywhere."

"Stop. Stop. I've heard enough. You two get in the car right now. Church begins in fifteen minutes."

Dire Straits

The store was going into dire straits and everyone knew it. But what was the answer? In the days following the blackout, the HeidtMoore made international news, "Lion Escapes the HeidtMoore During Madman Blackout," read one headline. *Women's Wear Daily*, the famed fashion-insider newspaper, was a little more incredulous: "HeidtMoore's Extravagance Cannot Survive as Sales Plummet amid Blackout." *The New York Times* headline simply stated, "It's Going to Take a Miracle to Keep the HeidtMoore Open."

♦

That Sunday, Mary, Samson and Deloris went to church. For Mary, this was becoming much less of a regular occurrence.

"*Mi hija*, you need to come to Mass with me more often," Deloris whispered to her daughter as she knelt down on the kneeler.

"Mama! Shhh!" Mary tried to hush her mother so that she could focus on her prayers. It was impossible. The thoughts of her adventures at work wouldn't allow her to be present. From Brandi's drinking problem and Sparkle's secret to directions and demands from Boggs and Sloan—not to mention the technology issues and the insane customers in the Children's department—the list seemed to go on and on.

"You need to tell your boss you cannot work on a Sunday."

There she was again. Why won't she drop it?

But in truth, Mary knew that she should probably go to Mass with her mother more and work less. It wasn't that she didn't want to attend church, but the hours at the store were grueling. Mary was required to work at least three Sundays a month and the one Sunday that she had free she wanted to spend with friends who were going to brunch and doing fun things. She knew that this time at Mass was not only important to her mother... she really did want to keep her faith strong as well. She had never not gone to church until she started working at the store. The more she found out about the HeidtMoore, the more she knew how important faith was. Keeping her father's catchphrase was a daily challenge. Yet she felt drawn to the wildness that each day offered. Mary felt more courageous each week. She was taking on more and more responsibility, even duties that were not part of her job description. She was also keenly aware that her paycheck seemed to be going right back to the store, as she looked down at the freshly pressed Dolce floral sheath dress.

Se-duc-tion

One of the more prominent customers to shop at the HeidtMoore was Mrs. Ivory. She was the wife of a Texas senator. Whenever she needed something for a big event, she always went to the HeidtMoore. With a well-publicized event coming up and a tight schedule to follow, she needed to place a handbag order to match the custom Christian Lacroix designer gown that she would be wearing. Tevi had assured her that it would not be a problem if she placed the order two weeks in advance of the event.

♦

"Goddammit! You said that I would have the damn boxes today! What you mean you ain't got no— Hold up. I have a customer comin'." said Ta'Keisha, a large African-American woman who was talking on the phone. Mrs. Ivory walked past the Cosmetics counter.

"Oh, hello! My name is Ta'Keisha. How may I assist you?"

"I am okay. Thank you."

"*THIS* is our new fragrance, Seduction, by Devinchy. That's right: *Seduction*. Just a little spray. Hold out your wrist." Ta'Keisha sprayed her wrist. She was going to make this sale.

"Now, you tell me you don't like the scent. Dang, it is *sexy* mama."

"Mmnn. Lives up to its name."

"Married? Single?"

"Pardon?"

"Girl! It don't matter. If you be single, that won't last long, wearing this scent. Married? You 'bout to get your man proposin' all over again. Damn. You be lucky if he even lets you out of the bedroom, let alone the house. Why don't you start with the small bottle until you be fully grown then you graduate to the larger one. Girl!!! You know I be messin'." Ta'Keisha burst out laughing. Mrs. Ivory was less amused. "I have to go.

Sorry. Maybe next time? I am late for my appointment upstairs." Mrs. Ivory continued her escape from Cosmetics.

Ta'Keisha got back on the phone. "You still there? Listen asshole, you said today. I cannot sell this Seduction shit without the lotion. Ya' hear me? Uh huh, no one messes with Ta'Keisha B!"

♦

No sooner had Mrs. Ivory left Ta'Keisha than she was approached by Zane.

"Hello. How are you today? Good. You have to have this special rejuvenating day cream. It reduces wrinkles in ten minutes, see? Look at my face?" Zane's face was perfectly smooth, like porcelain, although it was the result of plastic surgery and not the cream that he was selling. "I used it this morning. Hold out your hand. I won't take no for an answer!"

Mrs. Ivory held out her hand and Zane started rubbing her palm.

"This technique works like a charm... every time. See, wasn't I right? It feels amazing. What's your name, sweetie? My name is Zane and I can take care of you today."

"Actually...." Mrs. Ivory was looking around apprehensively.

"So what brings you in?"

"I—"

"You look so familiar! Has anyone told you that look a bit like Anne Hathaway? Adooore her. Oh my God. She was amazing in that film. What was it?"

"*The Dev—*"

"*Wears Prada*! Yes! Love! I could totally relate. Like, oh my God. When she, like, meets the guy, who is so hot, but then it turns out she should have been with the other one."

"It was—"

"Should we wrap up the 2.5-ounce or the 5-ounce? I can put it on your HeidtMoore card now."

"Um...."

"The 2.5-ounce is $990, but the 5-ounce is a much better deal. It's only $1,595. Which really is so much more given what you pay."

"I'll come back later."

"I don't know if it will be here later," Zane said with a sinister undertone in his voice.

"Really, I—"

"It could be all yours...." Zane was brutal. He wouldn't let her get a word in edgewise.

"I better go."

"You should not say no when you want to say yes." Mrs. Ivory practically ran past him, making a quick escape.

"Bitch," Zane muttered under his breath.

♦

Mrs. Ivory was just about to leave the Cosmetic department when another vendor approached her. This time it was Shirley, the seventy-five-year-old woman with a face made up of every product imaginable.

"Hiii, would you like to try some of this hand cream?"

Firmly, Mrs. Ivory responded, "Thank you. No. That man over there gave me a sample of his hand cream. I don't need any more."

"Zane? Oh... his cream is just fine. But you didn't buy some?"

"No! No, I didn't."

"I mean, it is fine and bless his little heart, he does a good job but, well... let me tell you about this." And Shirley began her selling spiel. "It is the finest hand cream that you will ever use. See? Just a small dab and you won't have any wrinkles. Not that you have wrinkles. Ha, ha, ha, ha... no. But one day, honey. This is imported, you know. And exclusive to the HeidtMoore." The exclusivity of this cream captured Mrs. Ivory's attention.

"Oh really? Aren't most of your products exclusive?"

"Many are. But this is the MOST exclusive. No one has this, and it was a great thing for the HeidtMoore to start selling this lotion. It has secret ingredients. The recipe has been kept in a family vault for centuries."

"How old is it?"

"The first lotion created was for... what was her name... Madam... Madame De Pompadour!"

"Old?"

"Real old."

"Where is it made? It says here... France."

"Oh nooo, honey. It's from Paris." Mrs. Ivory internally debated whether or not she should tell the vendor that Paris was in France.

"Well, thank you. Now, I must be going. I'm late. Goodbye."

♦

Mrs. Ivory stepped onto the winding escalator toward the Handbag department. She couldn't help but compare the associates in the Cosmetics department to the school of piranha that surrounded a beautiful guppy in the fish tank. Reaching the next floor, she saw Tevi and waved. "Do you have the swatch samples? I need to order now."

Talent Show

There was nothing like the annual HeidtMoore talent show for the employees, and this year it could not have come at a better time. After the active shooter, the blackout and rampant rumors about the HeidtMoore not being able to pay its electricity bills, the store needed a boost for morale.

The talent show was a time when associates could truly shine, to show their peers what they were really destined for.

The one man who loved it more than most was Sloan. It was because it was a part of HeidtMoore history.

"You mean I'm going to emcee the talent show?" Excited by the very idea of his fifth year as MC, Sloan could hardly contain himself.

"And Boggs? What is he doing this year?"

"Oh, you know, another shot at the piccolo." Brandi replied, turning her Yeti flask into a piccolo instrument.

"Oh Lord! Are you kidding? When is he *ever* going to retire that thing? We need to uplift the people, not depress them. As if the events of last month weren't traumatic enough. Jeez." Just when things couldn't get worse, his colleague insisted on playing his pathetic instrument. It was more than Sloan could handle.

Brandi took the lid off of her drink to take a sip.

"Sloan, be nice. He tries hard. Here." Brandi handed him the list. "I have the list of talents for you to look at."

He scanned the two-page list.

"What's this? Under name column is 'Ronnie,' then under the talent column is 'Douche.' Since when is that a talent?"

"Don't be grouchy. It's her specialty. It's actually a cute act."

"Who's scanning this? Oh no... how lovely." Sloan scrunched up his face. "Mandy in Customer Service is reciting *Romeo and Juliet*.

I can't wait."

"Stop being sarcastic. She's going to be wonderful."

"She's 45 years old and 250 pounds! I think the nurse would be better. Oh well. Sure. Whatever. I'll host this comedy of errors."

"You are the best. Thank you!"

Sloan returned her graciousness with a tight smile, thinking Mr. Heidt would be furious.

◆

It was showtime! For all of the effort and hoopla that was put into the talent show, one would think that it would be produced on an actual stage with proper lighting. But no, this show was set up in the grand Tea Room restaurant. Tables and chairs were shoved against the walls to create a "stage" and an ancient karaoke-style machine was brought in with a microphone that only worked sporadically.

"Next up, we have Mr. Boggs, giving his rendition of Adele's *Hello* on the, um...," it pained Sloan to read the list, "on the piccolo." He moved to the side to let Boggs take his position on center stage.

As Boggs approached the stage, Sloan shook his head in disbelief. Like an athlete about to compete, Boggs took several deep breaths and stretched awkwardly before taking out the piccolo from its case. With steely determination and focus, he put the instrument to his lips and started with the first couple of notes. It took a while before his instrument was in tune. Six long minutes later, the crowd applauded his performance.

Mary sat watching from the back of the room. She sat in confusion and amusement watching her boss and fellow colleagues perform. At the same time, it was kind of amazing that so many of them were actually really good. Who would have known? She was particularly impressed with Alfredo, the head of Housekeeping and Engineering, when he stood up and sang an aria from *Tosca*. He sang so beautifully. It literally took her breath away.

Other acts weren't quite as polished, such as the annual interpretive dance from Silwa in the Shipping department. Every year, costumed in a black leotard and spandex skirt, and with her hair wrapped in a turban, she performed the same dance. She swayed and made prayer hands to ancient African music for nearly five minutes. At the end, she was always crying. It was bewildering. It was very brave and something that Mary, the introvert that she was, would never do herself.

When Tanisha, the lead in Customer Service, came out dressed from head to toe in a black leather and latex catsuit with matching mask and long leather whip, no one was prepared for the "talent" which consisted of slithering around on the floor and doing a few twerks... no easy task in her five-inch stilettos.

Mary thought to herself, *This is a talent show, not an S&M club.*

"Who on earth is that?" Tevi asked Mary, as a small child appeared next to Catwoman.

"Her six-year-old," replied a random person sitting behind her who had overheard the comment.

Sure enough, a little boy was standing on the middle of the stage, looking more like a deer in headlights than an accomplice of Catwoman. Finally, out of fear of being sliced by the whip that Tanisha was brandishing, Sloan quickly introduced the next act. Tanisha purred and seductively flayed her whip in his direction, barely missing his ankles. Luckily, he had jumped up, missing it all together.

"That was certainly interesting. Thank you. Meow! The next act is Lulu and the Slingers, performing *'Till We Meet Again.'*"

The ancient group of Gift Galleries associates, led by Lulu, all came on stage dressed as World War II pinup girls while Bobby, the only man, was dressed as a fighter pilot.

While they got ready to sing, Mary looked around the room to see how many more acts were left. From the sidelines, Mary could see several associates waiting their turn, some nervously reciting lines or meditating. The acts that had already performed waited alongside the others: Boggs, polishing his piccolo; the Douche, looking deflated as she sat in a chair that was more like cabbage than a bathing item; and forty-five-year-old Juliet, checking her iPhone. There was also David in the Housekeeping department, practicing his magic tricks and dressed in a cape and black top hat.

"Now let me introduce the next one in our lineup this morning, Sparkle, who will be singing the Carpenters' *'Goodbye to Love.'* Take it away, Sparkle!"

A few claps were heard as Sparkle made her way to the front of the stage. Slowly she began....

"I'll say goodbye to love..."

"No one ever cared if I should live or die..."

The room was silent and uncomfortable. Sparkle's singing was shaky, although not terrible.

"Time and time again the chance for love has passed me by..."

"Story of my bloody life!" Tevi said.

"Gee, it's kind of depressing," Mary whispered to her.

"You have no idea. Being married to my husband and working in this dump. Yeah. It's depressing." Tevi loved to shock the new people and Mary was no exception.

"'*Goodbye to Love*?'" Mary questioned.

"Oh, you're talking about the song? That girl is a bloody nightmare." Then, suddenly, Tevi stood up and started clapping Sparkle off the stage.

"Thank you. That's good. Thank you. We've heard your great voice." Sitting back down, Tevi received disapproving looks from her peers. Addressing those around her, she said, "Well, someone has to take control and it's certainly not going to be that prat over there," referring to Sloan, who was at the side of the stage dabbing his eyes gently with a tissue. "Oh Christ! What a sap."

Sparkle, not knowing what to do, stood there in the spotlight like a wilted flower.

With a quiver in his voice, Sloan walked on stage. "That was very touching. Everyone, that was Sparkle. Now time for something else...."

While the next act was about ready to go on, Mary looked around the room and caught the eye of Nacho. Had he been watching her stare at Boggs and his piccolo? A dirty thought crossed her mind. She blushed. He smiled. She quickly turned toward Boggs again but all she could see was his hand going up and down the large, wooden, instrument. With a firm hold of his instrument, he moved slowly and gently then faster. Mary was flushed. She tried to shift her attention back to the talent show, but no... all she could do was think about... Nacho. She couldn't resist, she wanted one more look at him. This time, with a more seductive glow in her eyes, she looked back to see this magnetic man, the sexual tension pulsing through her. It was undeniably the most exciting feeling that Mary had ever experienced. She looked over, seductively biting her lower lip, but Nacho had gone.

"What the hell is the matter with you?" Tevi said in a measured and mocking tone. She was never one for sentimentality.

"Nothing!" Mary tried to act normal again.

"You're acting all weird and your face is red."

"No. Oh it's fine. It's a bit hot in here, that's all".

"It's never hot in here. It's bloody freezing. You have wet patches under your armpits too."

Suddenly, feeling very self-conscious, Mary stammered, "I do? Oh God." She could feel the wetness under her arms and the perspiration dripping down her face.

"Someone got you hot and bothered?"

What the heck, why can't she drop it? "No! It's nothing." Trying to be as convincing as possible, she quickly added, "I may be coming down with something."

"You're sick? Great. And she's sitting next to me. I'll be sick soon anyway, sick from watching all this crap. What's next on the program? Can we go home yet? I'm so bloody bored."

"Stop whining Tevi," whispered Lulu from behind, tapping Tevi on the shoulder.

"That concludes our annual talent show. Thank you everybody. Have a great day and sell lots. What do we say? 'Go get 'em, don't sweat 'em!'"

"Ha ha. 'Bit late for you, eh Mary?"

Everyone started shifting out of their seats and clearing out of the room. Nacho rushed up to Boggs as he was putting his piccolo away inside its velvet-lined case.

"We have a situation," said Nacho, with the intensity of leopard.

"We just finished the talent show. The store just opened. What could have possibly happened in two minutes? What's going on?"

"Mrs. Ivory, sir."

"Oh God. What's the matter?"

"She's come for the ostrich bag."

"The one-of-a-kind burgundy ostrich bag, the one where we have to capture the animal just for our top client, so that she can take it to the Governor's Ball tomorrow. Shit! Tomorrow's the Ball..."

"And we don't have the bag. She wants an explanation."

"Explanation? Yes, you know, we're gonna get the bag. Where's Sparkle? She's her client."

Tevi, overhearing the conversation on her way out of the room, mumbled to Mary as they walked out. "Bloody man, if he wasn't more interested in playing his piccolo and focused his attention on the client, he wouldn't be in this mess. But what do I know?" Tevi's cynicism knew no bounds.

"I don't think this is the time to be making catty remarks," said Zane, who was walking behind them.

"Hey, I tell it how it is. His brain is shit. I have a $22.5 million-dollar business, so I think I have the right to voice my opinion."

"Ladies and gentlemen, let's get to work now. Come along." Sloan was shooing them out of the restaurant.

The Custom Ostrich Bag

Mrs. Ivory was waiting very patiently in the Handbag department near the Fendi case line by the time the talent show had ended. She couldn't wait to see her brand-new purchase. As the Governor's wife, the event tomorrow was the biggest event of the year and the bag, the dress, and the matching shoes were all purchased on the premise that the bag would be in the store on time. Like Jackie Kennedy's pill box hat or Melania Trump's sky-high Louboutin heels, the handbag would play a very powerful role in the evening. It was a political weapon and Mrs. Ivory would pull out all of the stops if it meant getting her philandering husband voted back into office. The end game was the White House.

"Mrs. Ivory! What a lovely surprise. Welcome. How are you?" Boggs was doing his very best to act as if nothing was wrong.

"Marvelous. I can't wait to see the bag. You are so wonderful to get the bag for me. You do have it?"

"Er… yes. Oh, we have it! But first, why don't I show you our latest designs in Couture and find you a glass of champagne?"

"No thank you. Just the bag. I have so much to do today, you have no idea."

"Then you definitely need a glass of champagne! Just one. Won't hurt." He nodded in the direction of Sparkle and gestured for the champagne to be brought fourth.

"We have to get the bag from the back and so, in the meantime… let me introduce you to our…"—he caught the eye of Chef, who was passing by—"chef." He spoke the last word in a tone loud enough to command his attention.

"Yes," said Chef, walking over.

"You have the meal prepared for our very special guest, don't you?" Before he could say a word, Boggs continued egging him on. "And you will be accompanying her to the dining room."

"But I didn't order food?"

"We are here to make sure everything that you desire is ready for you. Think of it as part of our care package for clients who we adore."

"In that case, my goodness! I am flattered."

"Chef will show you through to the dining room. It's just a thank you for purchasing your beautiful handbag."

"If you say so, Chief." Chef never missed a beat, particularly when a beautiful, rich, older woman was involved. Boggs gestured for her to walk ahead and took the opportunity to whisper in to Chef's ear.

"Whatever you do, make it spectacular. Champagne, caviar, the works. And put on that charm. We're in the middle of a crisis right now. I'll fill you in later."

"Sure, but what the hell is going on? I dunno if the caviar even came in with the shipment this morning."

"Think of something. Anything. I just... I need a little time to figure this out." Chef took Mrs. Ivory's arm and escorted her to the restaurant on the fourth floor.

Boggs's head was spinning. He had to figure this out. *There wasn't any time.* "Shit. Fuck. Shit. Fuck. Fuck. Fuck. Fuckity fuck fuck." he muttered to himself as he walked back to the cage. He slammed his hand down on the tiny, flimsy desk inside the small storage closet. This remarkably claustrophobic room served as the gazillion-dollar-producing Handbag office. Boggs hit the white plastic desk harder than he meant to and the whole setup fell to the ground.

"Crap." He bent down to collect the papers, various sales reports and floor plans, that had been scattered on the floor, completely out of order. As he tried to straighten up the mess, he realized that times like this were when he was very thankful that he was an executive and not a manager anymore. The conditions were not suitable for a man of his stature. Tevi entered and couldn't believe the mess that her manager had made.

"Boggs! Hi. What are you doing down there?"

◆

While Mrs. Ivory was at her lunch, specially prepared for her by Chef, Tevi and Sparkle were frantically trying to figure out what to do about the missing bag. They walked into the executive offices to discuss with Boggs what to do next. T barely noticed them come in, as she was deep in a phone conversation.

"I understand, Ta'Keisha. I will let you know as soon as I hear anything."

Beside her desk was a large rolling rod of clothes, shoes and bags—including the one-of-a-kind Ferraeny—with a giant sign that read "Hudson Hawn."

"T, we won't be back after the shoot. Here is the list of what we are taking," said Vivian giving T the list.

T glanced over the list, looked at the rod and then signed off on it. "Looks good, just make sure you give the list to security on your way out."

"Will do. See you tomorrow. Thank you."

"Boggs there?" Before T could reply, Boggs yelled from his office. "T, get me Tevi."

"She's right here."

"Can you ask her to come in?" Why he had to ask T this question when Tevi could hear everything, T had no idea. Tevi and Sparkle walked into Boggs's office to find Boggs, sitting back in a swivel chair cross-legged, pointing his finger like a pistol at Tevi.

"Shoot."

"I already bloody explained it to you on the phone."

Boggs paused to think. "So, let me get this straight. We don't have the exotic for Mrs. Ivory? And we don't have an ostrich handbag? There's not a single one in the store?"

"No, it's being made. And I did not promise the customer anything. She just showed up this morning. And the fucking bag isn't due until next week."

Curious, the store monkey, popped out from underneath Boggs's desk chewing on some peanuts. Sparkle became distracted by Curious, which made Tevi even more frustrated.

"Hey. Easy. We don't need that kind of language."

"She can get very angry and it is not going to be pretty if we don't come up with a solution."

"We are known for solutions. We make miracles happen every day. Let's just put our thinking caps on. The HeidtMoore is known for miracles."

"It's useless." On days like this, Tevi wondered why she ever got into retail in the first place.

"Useless? No no, Tevi. It isn't useless. We at the HeidtMoore do not believe in uselessness. We have a system in place. You must trust the system. The system works. You must have hope. That is our job." Boggs sat back in his chair and crossed his legs. He had an odd confidence about him that made Tevi uneasy. "So, you have checked that we don't have any bags which are similar?"

Tevi looked at Sparkle, who started frantically clicking her pen, making an annoying noise.

"No, there are no similar bags."

"So, the question is, what would you do if you were a customer who was promised a $40,000 handbag?"

Tevi and Sparkle looked at each other again. Sparkle looked as if she was seriously considering this question. Finally, Tevi spoke up. "I would murder the man who is, right now, running this department store."

Boggs chuckled to himself. "Ha! That's me." He paused as he realized that the joke was on him. "Wait. That's not funny." He readjusted his sitting position. "Look. We don't have a bag that's similar. And she is not leaving without a handbag."

Pointing at Tevi again, Boggs made an executive decision.

"Okay, I'm calling the Buying office to see if there is another one." Pressing the speaker button, he dialed an extension. "Buying office please. Uh huh, yes. Carlton."

"Carlton here." A nasally East-Coast accent came on the other end. The rich, debonair demeanor that the man's voice portrayed was more than Tevi could handle. She grabbed Sparkle in an attempt to leave the office.

"Carlton, we have a situation here. Do you recall the Ferraeny bag order? The ostrich one."

"Yes. It's one-of-a-kind. As I recall, hers is being made now."

"The customer is here now."

"Too bad. Nothing I can do. It's out of my hands. There is only one other like it and it's being used."

"Is there anything you can do to rush the order? She has already purchased it."

"Aside from dragging the ostrich to slaughterhouse myself and slapping on some red velvet color, she'll just have to wait." "Carlton, she is going to want a refund if we don't do something. We cannot take a $40,000 return. Help us out."

"Let me see what I can do. I have connections with *Vogue Italia* and maybe they have one. Let me check and I will get back to you."

"Today?"

"Heavens no. They're in Italy. It's 9:00pm there."

Boggs hit the speaker button and accidentally knocked the receiver off of the hook. Clicking his fingers, he called out for T.

"*T!!! COME IN HERE!*"

"Yes, I'm here," T said quietly, already standing at his door.

"Get... get... what's the guy's name? The one we use for handbags. For all of the repairs that we do. You know... what is his name?"

"You mean Stan?"

"Yep. That's it. Stan. Great guy. Put me through to him, would you?"

"Sure." Why she had to be called into Boggs's office for this, she had no idea. He was like a child.

T, back at her desk, dialed Stan. As soon as she had Stan on the line, she patched the call through to Boggs's office.

Boggs's red light was blinking, indicating that the call was coming through. He pressed the speaker button.

"Stan! My man."

◆

In a factory that looked more like an auto body shop in South Dallas, Stan surveyed his team of about fifty workers. No HeidtMoore employee ever visited Stan's, as it was called. For good reason too. The work floor resembled a sweatshop and Stan's office, located on a mezzanine overlooking his overworked and stressed-out employees, was smoky and cluttered.

Standing about five feet in height—give or take a few inches and depending on whether or not he was wearing his custom-made platform shoes—Stan was an overweight bald man of sixty. Originally from Brooklyn, he had moved to Dallas to escape a few bad dealings with the Mafia. He set himself up in his new city with a custom repair shop and went about charming everyone and anyone in Dallas. He was the sort of man who could sell ice to an Eskimo. He was a brilliant salesman who had been married five times and maintained control of one of the most secretive operations in Dallas. No one really knew what went on behind the doors of Stan's.

Small streams of sunlight filtered through the discolored plastic blinds in an otherwise dark and dusty room. Stan's desk faced a window that made up the wall, overlooking his workers. The setup always gave Stan the capability to watch over the action below. It also allowed the minimum amount of energy from Stan, since he could speak to them via the speaker system that he had installed.

Sitting at his desk, Stan smoked a large cigar while he listened to Boggs explain the predicament that he was in.

"Sorry to her that. Sounds like it would have been a great bag."

"That's where you come in, Stan. We would like you to make a replica."

"Ah jeez... That's a tall order, Boggs."

"Please! You have to. She's currently having lunch in the restaurant but we can't keep her there all day. We can't stall much longer."

"Let me see what I can do." The two men talked some more, and Boggs sent over a picture of the bag so that Stan could get precise measurements.

"Yep, yep... uh huh... I have it. Let me put you on hold. One moment."

Stan turned to the window and turned on the speaker, then screamed to the workers below in near-perfect Mandarin: "Listen! We have an order for an ostrich bag. See this bag? You make this now. What are you gonna do? Yeah, that's right. Stop everything and make this bag. Get to work!"

The disgruntled workers below returned to work, focusing on their new order.

"Boggs. It's done. You can count on us. We got this in the bag." As he coughed and spluttered, Stan put the phone down. "No pun intended. Ciao."

Boggs couldn't be happier. It was a miracle and yet another affirmation that Boggs should be running the HeidtMoore. Boggs called down to the Handbag counter to speak to Tevi, excited to share the news about the handbag. She answered the phone.

"Hello, handbags, this is Tevi speaking."

"Tevi, I've got a bag coming. We just need a couple of hours. Keep her busy: take her to the salon, show her the animals in the windows, let her play with Curious. Do whatever it takes."

◆

Tevi walked over to the restaurant. Mrs. Ivory had already been there for two hours. It was probably time to check on the client.

Tevi entered the lilac-colored restaurant, a definite throwback to the 1950s. She spotted Mrs. Ivory, Chef, and a chilled bottle of Veuve Clicquot. They were seated at a table in the corner of the room. *A bit intimate, wasn't it?* She walked over to the table.

"Mind if I join you?"

"Please take a seat. Chef was just telling me all about his new recipe. It sounds divine."

"Mrs. Ivory, you are the most delightful woman I've ever met. I'll cook for you anytime." Chef refilled their champagne glasses.

If looks could kill, Tevi would have had Chef dead at that very moment.

◆

Standing at the LP window, a scrawny delivery man was tapping the glass, trying to get Nacho's attention.

"I have delivery. I have delivery."

Opening up the glass protector window, Nacho took the piece of paper from the man to sign. "You have a delivery for who? What is it?" Knowing full well what it was, Nacho never put anything to chance when it came to security.

"I have package for... Boggy."

"Hold on." Nacho called the Operations department. "Yeah, there is a package here for Boggs."

The delivery man handed over the bag to Willy, who appeared immediately. "Thank you. Thank you. Thank you very much." He bowed to both men, then shuffled off.

"Willy, take this to the fifth floor immediately. Do not let it out of your sight."

"You got it, Chief." And off Willy went.

♦

T looked up from her computer upon seeing Willy. She couldn't conceal her grimace.

"Hey beautiful." Willy stood still, staring at T.

"Just gimme the damn bag." T grabbed it from him but wasn't quick enough to escape his fingers from caressing her hand. "You do that one more time and I swear—"

"T, is that the bag?" Boggs jumped out from his office.

"Yes Boggs, I have it."

"Awesome! Keep it there. I'm calling the crew now."

Moments later, T, Boggs, Tevi, and Sparkle were standing around T's desk with anticipation. Boggs slowly unwrapped the package, pulling out... a hideous bright-blue bag.

"What the fuck! This is not burgundy," exclaimed Tevi. "I don't even think this is a Ferraeny. This is... this is aquamarine monkey-piss blue! Mrs. Ivory ordered *burgundy*."

Boggs was stunned and Tevi was in disbelief. T looked pained. Sparkle was clicking her pen.

"It's supposed to be the burgundy ostrich bag." Tevi said, matter-of-factly.

"Wait! I saw that same bag in burgundy earlier. I signed off on it. It's at the shoot. I'm positive that's the one."

"What!? T, are you sure? Not a problem. T, where is the shoot?"

"Candy Creek."

"That's two hours away! Still, not a problem. Where are my keys?"

"Boggs, you have a meeting with Ta'Keisha about the inventory problem."

"Ah, that's right. Okay. Why don't you go then. Make sure someone from Security goes with you. *Now.* Hurry." Boggs picked up phone to call Security. "Oh hi, Nacho. I need you to go with T to retrieve an item on a shoot at Candy Creek. It is urgent."

"Urgent? I—"

T cut him off. "Are you kidding? I can't. I have to get this inventory report to Corporate."

"You can do that later."

"You know I can't have overtime. I have to do it now. Someone else will have to go."

"Okay, who is the closing manager on duty?" T glanced at the schedule posted on the cork board adjacent to her desk. "Mary is the closing manager here today."

"Then she will have to go. Call her now."

Candy Creek

Mary was slightly dumbfounded by the predicament that she was in. On the one hand, she couldn't believe her luck, sitting there with Nacho. On the other, she couldn't believe that she was once again called to do a task that had absolutely nothing to do with her job. But there she was, cruising in Nacho's hot rod. Staring out the window. Then staring at Nacho. Then staring straight ahead. Then glancing at him again. And so on. Then their eyes met. She quickly turned away.

Nacho broke the silence. "So, this bag is pretty important, I guess." He fully knew how urgent it was.

"Oh God, yes. You would not believe the drama that has gone on over this bag. All day long. I heard even the President of the United States is involved."

They both sat in silence for a moment, pondering how the President might be involved.

"Huh." That was all Nacho had to say.

"Thank you for driving."

"I had no choice. It's important and someone's gotta do it."

"Well, it's—" She had not finished her sentence before Nacho reached out to touch her arm.

"Hey, my pleasure."

Feeling very flustered, Mary turned away, trying to be as professional as possible. *Why did he have to do that?* Nacho was obviously trying to make an effort.

"Do you like being in the store? You've been here, what, six months?"

"Not bad! You know, I like it. I mean, it's different than what I thought the job would be." Feeling uncomfortable, she really wanted to know more about him. "What about you? How is Security? Where were you before this?"

"You know, I came from a correctional facility."

"Oh!?" That was not what she was expecting.

"The funny thing is... I dealt with criminals. The place was a zoo, an absolute madhouse. The wild, crazy and insane were there, and now I am in luxury retail—at the best department store in the country—and I am STILL dealing with crazy people. And it can feel like a zoo."

They both laughed. Mary relaxed a little more.

"A correctional facility. Whoa. That is... that is... what was that like?" Mary was at a loss for words. If it turned out that Nacho was a reformed criminal, she wasn't sure she could handle it.

"Yep. I managed 6,000 inmates. It could get intense. Kind of like the HeidtMoore."

"Tell me about it!" Then came the moment that she longed for.

"But I get to work with some great people. Like you."

Was he flirting with her? *Stay cool.* She could feel her face becoming hot. She could also feel drops of perspiration forming under her arms again. *How embarrassing!* And even worse, the song on the radio was Otis Redding's *"These Arms of Mine."*

♦

By the time Mary and Nacho got to Candy Creek, the director of the photo shoot was giving notes to a couple of models while the crew arranged the HeidtMoore animal brigade.

As they watched, it became obvious that the director was telling the model what she would be doing in the upcoming photo session. The cameraman and photographers were preparing and adjusting two boats on the lake. The model was about to proceed with her action shot of tossing the bag overboard while jumping from one boat to the other.

"Look! There it is. What are they doing?" Mary nudged Nacho to look toward the model but his eyes were on the rest of the crew. The cameraman gave the nonverbal cue to proceed and the director shouted in to the megaphone.

"Come on, Cindy! Now as you are jumping, drop the bag. You are angry. You are upset. He's an ass. Remember that, Cindy. An ass! I need emotion. Emotion. Cindy!"

"No way. They aren't...?"

"Yep. But not on our watch they aren't."

"What are you going to do?"

"Watch out." Nacho suddenly broke into a sprint, yelling back at Mary, "I got this." His voice trailed off the faster he ran. He jumped over camera bags and zigzagged around rolling rods, sprinting toward the bag on the lake. Then, as if in slow-motion, Nacho did a triple long jump right as the bag fell from the model's hands. He was able to catch it before it hit the water.

Mary stood in awe watching what had just happened. Her hero. The cameraman and models stood around, disgusted. Taking the precious item over to Mary in his dripping wet clothes, Nacho shouted back to the crew. "Folks, we are taking this back to the store."

The hour and half back to the store was one of Mary's best moments ever. She and Nacho talked and giggled. They found out more about each other. She hoped that it would not be the last time.

◆

Mary and Nacho got back to the store and Nacho promptly gave the bag to Tevi, who ran over to Mrs. Ivory, who was sobering up with an espresso in the French Café.

"Here you go. You see, it's perfect!"

"Thank you, Tevi. I don't know what I would do without you," said Mrs. Ivory, completely unaware of what the store had gone through to get her the bag.

"It was nothing. We are looking forward to seeing you at the Hudson Hawn PA." Tevi brushed off the compliment as if it was nothing.

Standing at a distance so Tevi could have her moment of glory, Mary and Nacho couldn't believe it. They looked at each other shaking their heads. Now it was time to let Boggs know that the mission had been accomplished. Nacho called Boggs.

"Boggs, mission complete."

"Thank you, Nacho. Amazing. Great job. Unbelievable."

Putting the phone down, Nacho motioned for Mary to leave with him. "Gonna grab a coffee. Want something?" Mary smiled. Nacho glanced down at his Rolex and casually checked the time. "Or how about a drink? It's almost the end of the workday anyway."

"Sure.   I'd   love   to."

Flirty Birds

Mary and Nacho met at Flirty Birds, a bar down the street from the HeidtMoore. The professional crowd gathered there for the Happy Hour specials.

"Do you come here often?" Mary innocently asked Nacho. *Oh my God, what am I thinking? Who says that?!*

"I've been here once with a buddy of mine from work."

"Oh goodness. Sorry, that sounded like such a pickup line."

He laughed a little. "No, you're fine. Can I... what can I get you? It says here on the menu that the margaritas are good."

"I'll take a margarita."

"We'll make that two. I'll be right back." Nacho walked up to the bar.

It was an awkward start to the evening and the more natural Mary tried to be, the more she tensed up and her muscles tightened. *What could one drink hurt?*

"Thanks."

Mary knew that her mother would kill her if she knew she was drinking tequila after work with the head of Security. Her mother had a saying, "*Mi amor*, tequila makes your clothes fall off." Nothing of the sort would happen here. Or would it? The drinks arrived and they sat down at a table by the window. This was going to be a wonderful evening... if she could ever relax.

Unfortunately for Mary, it was destined to be short-lived. Outside the window, Mary spotted the executive team and several managers from the HeidtMoore heading toward the bar.

"Hey, yo, what do we got here!" Boggs yelled upon entering the bar, while the rest of the team descended on their table. He was followed by Pietro, who promptly ordered a wine spritzer from a passing waitress. Looking past the visual manager, Mary saw Brandi and Vivian, who soon took seats beside Mary.

"Oh man! I'm starving." Vivian stated.

"I just need a drink." Brandi grabbed a waiter. "Could I have a double vodka with a splash of soda?"

"And I will take the chicken and waffles with a rum and Coke." Vivian had ordered without even looking at the menu.

Pietro brushed off a seat before sitting down. "Oh, I'll just take the *crudité*." Turning to the group, he said, "I'm on a strict diet. It's just ghastly. And Mary, what do you do."

"I'm the Children's manager."

T arrived and was about to place an order at the bar when Brandi yelled out. "Hey T! Come over here. Sit here."

Nacho leaned over to Mary. "You know I didn't invite them."

"It's fine." Mary was trying to stay calm. She took a sip of her drink.

"A round of shots for the table," Boggs shouted to the waiter as he returned with Vivian and Brandi's orders. Everyone cheered, except for Nacho and Mary.

An hour later and two rounds of tequila in, Boggs's partner Rod joined the group and was soon entertaining the intoxicated crowd with stories of their relationship. By the time that round three of shots came, Mary could barely move her mouth. She was suffering from the rare, debilitating condition known as lockjaw. Without the ability to move her mouth, Mary somehow had to communicate that maybe it was time that she left. Grabbing a napkin, she wrote down that she was leaving. Then she passed it to Nacho.

In the parking lot Nacho gave Mary a gentle hug goodbye and said, "Sorry about your lockjaw. See you tomorrow?"

Mary nodded and got into her car.

Night Shift

Nacho was headed out of town for a few days off. It was rare for managers to receive multiple days off in a row, so he was excited.

"Guys, got everything? Remember, you need anything, you call. Okay? I don't want any shenanigans while I'm gone, okay? I'm leaving you in charge of a large operation here and I do not want anything going wrong. I'll be back in a few days. Remember, you need me, you got my number."

"Yes. We got it. Enough already. Don't worry. Nothing is going to go wrong. Bye!"

Slinging his backpack over on shoulder, Nacho finally left the office, leaving Danny and Brad in charge of Loss Prevention.

"Damn, why he gotta be that way? For fuck's sake, we're not babies."

"Finally, we got the place all to ourselves."

"Dude, you're so creepy and weird."

It was just a typical night hanging out in the Loss Prevention office of the HeidtMoore, except that the big boss, Nacho, wasn't there. Each of the thirty screens surveying the store showed the various departments, quiet and peaceful with the lights dimmed. The only action was the movement of the housekeeping staff, who were currently dusting off fixtures and preparing the store for another day.

The security office itself was somewhat of a frat house. The only thing missing was a group of beer cans littering the room. Danny was from the Bronx and had worked in Loss Prevention for ten years. His first job was as a car salesman at a dealership there that was run by the mob. Then there was Brad, a good ol' boy from Texas with no ambition or aspirations of moving up in the world. The two of them were excited to work the night shift without the supervision of Nacho. This was possibly the easiest of jobs because there was nothing going on. It was a time to shoot the shit and pig out on junk food... something that Nacho would never allow.

"Hey. You watch that game last night?"

"Ah, dude! That play! I couldn't believe it."

"Yeah, for real. Good pitch on the inner part of the plate though, right?"

"Are you kidding? Trumbo is the shit."

"Not as good as Fielder though. C'mon!"

"Seriously? Fielder fucking *sucked* in the last inning."

"Hey, you gonna eat that thing, or what? If you don't, I will."

"*BURRITOooooo! 'Coz I only YOLOoooo...*," Brad sang, placing the burrito on a paper plate and putting it in the microwave. He pressed the start button a couple of times, trying to get it to work.

"We gotta get a new one of these. This button gets jammed."

"Yo! Come here. Hello? What is this?"

Leaving the burrito cooking in the microwave, Brad walked back to the monitors.

"Is she? What is she doing!?"

"It looks... like... she is—"

"Dude! Who does she think she is? Selena?" Brad chuckled.

Up on the third floor was Gloria, the cleaner for Fine Apparel. She had no idea that she was being watched by Security. Lost in her own world, vacuuming in and around the fixtures, she swayed gently to the beat of the song currently playing on her radio, a small set from Radio Shack. It wasn't much but it helped her escape the pressures of her day-to-day existence, cleaning and dusting the HeidtMoore and mopping the restrooms. Being an illegal immigrant, this wasn't her dream job, but she would do whatever it took to build a better life for herself and her family. She had six mouths to feed at home and also needed to send money to her brothers and sisters back in Mexico.

It was some ten years ago that Gloria had crossed the border and found herself at the storefront of the HeidtMoore begging for money. She had nothing except her small children and a giant, empty cardboard box. That was when she was noticed by Mr. Heidt himself. She had worked for him ever since.

"*Una loba en el armario. Tiene ganas de salir. Deja que se coma el barrio. Antes de irte a dormir.*" Gloria's favorite Shakira song, "*Loba*," was playing. She loved this song! "*There's a she wolf in the closet....*" Gloria picked up the feather duster and, using the wooden end as a microphone, started writhing across the floor, singing into the stick and imagining herself to be a supremely sexy diva. She had never done it before, but tonight she was feeling more daring. Who would notice if she took the dazzling necklace off of the mannequin closest to the balcony? She would only wear it for a minute. She wasn't doing anything wrong. Gloria undid the clasp of the quartz-and-emerald necklace and placed it carefully around her neck. *Wow! What a beautiful piece of jewelry.*

Meanwhile, Danny and Brad were not paying any attention to the monitor.

"Dude, why do you have to be so racist? I'm gonna tell Nacho that he hired a racist."

"That is so childish. What is racist about what I said?"

"Why couldn't you say Madonna or someone?"

"Who the fuck says Madonna? You are so frigging *guido*, you know that?"

"Whatever. Okay, that hot chick married to Tim McGraw then. What's her name?"

"Faith. Oh, I don't think she is trying to be like Faith, Madonna, Lady Gaga, or whoever. She got moves." Impersonating the cleaning woman impersonating a singer, Brad started moving about the LP office with an exaggerated swagger and a hip thrust.

"Ah, dude! You're crazy. Hey—" Danny sniffed the air and scrunched up his nose. "Hey!" Brad, oblivious, continued doing his dance. "What is that smell? Did you fart? It smells like burnt beans."

"No! Of course not!" He was offended that Danny would even suggest such a thing.

"Dude, for real. What is that?"

"Shit. Shit! My burrito is on fire!"

"Damn it! Dumbass. Quick, unplug it."

Brad was almost knocked over by the billowing smoke as he unplugged the microwave. He gingerly pulled out what was left of his dinner, now nothing but a charred toothpick sticking out of a solid brown and yellow lump. The melted cheese and black beans were dripping onto the floor.

"Oh shi-it."

While the burning burrito commotion was going on, Gloria put the necklace back on the mannequin where it belonged. It was time to wrap up and go home. She untied her apron, picked up her case of cleaning supplies and turned back one last time toward the necklace. But it wasn't there. Where was it? Gloria panicked and searched the mannequin, but didn't see anything. Should she report it? No, they would think it was her. She could go to jail or worse... get deported. She took a few deep breaths, said a Hail Mary and decided to walk away as if nothing had happened.

It must have been around midnight when the necklace disappeared from sight, having slipped through a hole in the floor and landing three floors   down.

Shop Heist

And there it wasn't. An $8,000 necklace was missing from a mannequin and the only explanation as to why Security hadn't seen it disappear was a burnt burrito.

"You've got to be kidding me!?" Boggs was infuriated. Brad stood there helplessly along with his equally sheepish partner.

"Well? What do you have to say for yourselves?" Neither one could reply.

"That's what I thought. Let's review tape. Come on." With shaky hands, Brad rewound the security footage of the previous night's events. What they saw on the tape was a cleaning lady singing into her mop.

"But she isn't near the Precious Jewels case. Give me footage of that."

Danny's footage of the Precious Jewelry department wasn't recorded. They were so focused on the singing lady and the burning burrito that they completely forgot to turn on the tape. *Oh brother. This was not going to go down well.* Danny and Brad needed an alibi.

"Danny?"

"So, er... look closely at the footage. See this *chica* has that mop and she moves it. You think she can't get a necklace out of here? It's a clever trick. Who would assume that a necklace is tucked behind a cleaning mop?"

The men looked closer at the footage, leaning in closer to the monitor.

"I bet she's part of one of those crazy MS-13 gangs coming cross the border. Betcha."

"Men. Good work. We aren't gonna be intimidated."

All of a sudden, and without needing to review any further tape, Boggs had his culprit.

"Who is she? We are about to find out. Call her in. Now!" There was a hint of menace in his voice.

♦

Off went Brad and Danny. They were a bit like the two stooges, clumsily making their way out of the door to find the unsuspecting cleaning lady.

They found her on the second floor, putting away her mop and taking off her apron. Danny stood in front of the scared woman. He opened the door to the closet, taking out the cleaning mop.

"Yeah, we'll be taking this."

"Follow us, please." Being as authoritative as possible, Brad wished that this could be over quickly. They walked back down to the Loss Prevention office, where Boggs was waiting impatiently. She stood there mystified. Why was she in Security? She was a good girl, making a decent living, trying the best that she could.

"Sit down." Boggs started the interrogation.

"Where were you last night at about midnight?" He continued in an unusually stern voice. There was a moment of silence before the woman finally responded, with no clue of what she had just been asked.

"*¿Cómo? No entiendo.*"

"Where were you?!" Boggs said in an even louder voice, as if this was the secret to making the Mexican woman understand him.

"I said... *¿Dónde estás, señorita?*"

She was very confused by this man. Then she said the answer that she thought he wanted to hear.

"*¿Aquí?*"

"No. I meant... *la noche*!!!"

"*No sé. ¡No sé!*" She was pleading with him.

"Damn it! This is useless. Play the tape again, men."

The guys played back the tape. Watching herself on the small TV monitor, the cleaning lady started crying. This was terrible. They all watched her sing and dance when she should have been cleaning the floor and doing her work.

"Hey! Stop that! Tell us about the necklace. Where is it? You can't fool us with your crying...."

She cried harder. Boggs eventually felt pity for her. Conflicted by the need to seek justice with stern punishment and the desire to calm her down, he could no longer be mad at the poor weeping woman who was quivering before him like a shaking leaf. In an act of compassion, he put one arm on her shoulder.

"Hey now, you're alright. Don't cry. Please. There's no need to do that."

They had filmed her dancing and singing. *What creeps!* Gloria uttered "*Tu cara parece un payaso.*" Loosely translated, it meant "you look like a clown."

"I know. I know. It's okay. Calm down, alright?"

"*Creo que eres un gran culo peludo.*" "I believe that you are a hairy ass."

She was feeling a little better about the situation knowing that no one in the interrogation room could speak or understand a word of Spanish.

"Boggs, it wasn't her."

"We've looked at every inch of the mop and nothing."

"Nope. Doesn't look like it. Then who the hell was it? Okay. You can leave now." The cleaning lady sat there.

"Go on. Go. ¡*Vámanos*!"

"*Peludo,*" she muttered as she walked out the door. Unbeknown to Boggs, he was being called an ass.

Pietro's Vision

Around the store, lights were being turned on, registers opened and employees trickled in for their shifts. At the far end of the Men's department, an artsy group stood analyzing and critiquing the newly installed statue of Mr. Heidt, Jr.

"I mean, it's fine, but do we really need the essence of Heidt here in this spot? He needs more exposure." The head of Visual, Pietro, the gay Italian, was known for his expertise in hanging store paintings and flamboyant visual displays. He was also as well-known for his many affairs with the men working in Cosmetics.

"I like it. He looks hot." Pietro ignored one of his team's more adolescent comments.

"Does the sculpture give energy to the space? Does it inspire? One must always ask the question."

"I just feel that we need more bronze, less alabaster. We need more richness in the area." Another colleague had spoken up, as if the surrounding gold finishes covering the cash wraps weren't enough.

"Good point. But let's not suffocate the area. One cannot lead a camel to water when he is already wading through an ocean. We need texture."

"There will be texture if we match Heidt with the tartan fabrics of the latest season."

"Brilliant idea. What are the colors of the tartan of the coming season?"

"On the runway, we're showing the Cornwall in a mustard hue."

Pietro didn't really know what that was. But he was a fond believer of the motto, "fake it till you make it."

"That could be a very interesting. What else?"

"What about the MacTavish? It is a stunning piece. Blood red, peacock blue."

"Origin?"

"Comes from the great Scottish clan, the MacTavish, dating back to at least 1355. It's a fabulous tie-in to the Hudson Hawn PA."

"Wow. Where do you find this shit? That's like, so old." The younger member of the staff had chimed in. *No filter whatsoever.*

"Keep going. A crest? Coat of arms?"

"Yes. A boar's head. So cool. Really neat."

"I got it. We need to have the statue draped in this MacTin tartan."

"MacTavish."

"Yes. That's what I said."

"I think that it's a shitty piece of tin," one of the assistants whispered to a coworker standing in their circle.

"We make Mr. Heidt a sort of bronze god—a noble character, some sort of medieval king—defeating the tyrants trying to upset his power and kingdom."

It was all about creating a fantastical story. Making people believe and aspire to something that they thought was impossible.

"I get it. He is the ruler and in the Men's department."

"Every man should walk in this department a peasant and leave a king. Yes! Let's move on to the Fine Apparel department so that we can continue discussing the setup for Hudson Hawn."

These types of visual meetings were not uncommon at the HeidtMoore. It could take hours to discuss the visual effectiveness of moving a fixture from one side of a register to the other. All considerations had to be observed: spatial contrast sensitivity, breathing room, visual weight, and, finally, selling potential. Every action of the visual team was weighed heavily. They moved as a unit, sort of like a traveling band of hippies.

Reaching the Fine Apparel department on the fifth floor, Pietro tripped over a loose piece of floor tile.

"These floors are wretched."

"It's loose—"

"Nightmare."

"I could have died. Someone call Alfredo, the engineer, and have him get this fixed."

"Hey! What have you uncovered?"

In unison, each member of the visual tribe bent down to observe the discovery. Pietro pushed aside another loosened tile to find a large hole, big enough to hold an ostrich egg.

"My God! This is a death trap!" Unbeknownst to the group, there had been a mannequin near the hole in the floor which had recently been moved by Loss Prevention during reconnaissance over the missing necklace. But did the security team find the hole? *Of course not.* It was the   visual   team.

Linda Langley

In preparation for the upcoming personal appearance, Channel 5 News had contacted T for a story. T had passed the message on to Mr. Heidt but, being apprehensive about reporters since the completely fictional story about an affair that he had had with an associate, he never responded. Now that he was out of the country for a month, T had to choose between Boggs and Sloan.

The phone rang.

"Thank you for calling the HeidtMoore, Executive Office, how may I assist you today?"

"Yes, this is Linda Langley. I'm calling to confirm the interview with Channel 5 tomorrow."

"Oh yes. Hello, Ms. Langley. Mr. Heidt is traveling but Mr. Boggs, one of our Assistant General Managers, will be doing the interview with you. He has been with the HeidtMoore for years and will give you a lovely tour of our store. He knows all of the ins and outs of this magnificent place."

"Fantastic! Does 6:00am still work? Our crew will arrive before the store opens and stay the full day to speak with both customers and associates, if that is okay."

"Shouldn't be a problem. Thank you, Ms. Langley."

"Linda, please! No, thank you. The HeidtMoore is legendary. This story will take our channel to the top of Sweeps Week. We are so excited. Thank you again and see you tomorrow!"

Linda Langley was the top news anchor in the city. Somewhat of a celebrity, she was well-known for breaking the most eventful stories. She was polished and poised, always wearing the latest designer suits available at the HeidtMoore. She shopped with Patrick in the Fine Apparel department but, of course, never actually came into the store. Many rumors swirled about that Mr. Langley preferred Patrick to the Mrs., though it was very hush-hush.

♦

Boggs had not slept well the night before. He and Rod had had an argument which had kept them both up late and ultimately in separate bedrooms. Trying to push it aside, Boggs thought about the interview. It really was a dream come true. *Forget that it was local television*. This was his chance to show everyone what a true leader he was. So there he stood, behind the huge gold doors of the main entrance, waiting for Linda Langley and her crew. He could see himself in the reflection and straightened his tie. *You are a star.*

Linda and her crew arrived and started setting up. With the push of a button, the massive doors began to slide open. Boggs pictured himself on a stage for a moment. *Showtime, Boggs.* A terrifying sound was heard, a click followed by a hummm. The doors to the outside stopped.

"What the fuck! This isn't supposed to happen," he mumbled. There, in front of him, was Linda, mouthing through the gap.

"Do we need a special password?"

"Ms. Langley, we only require a HeidtMoore credit card...."

As if by magic, upon the words "HeidtMoore," the doors resumed opening.

The crew set up and their bright lights were everywhere. *5, 6, 7, 8....* Boggs had a flashback to the days when he and his team of cheerleaders were jumping up and down during competitions. *Those were the days.*

"So nice to see you, Mr. Boggs! This interview is history in the making!" *She had no idea.* "The HeidtMoore is legendary," Linda continued before Curious, appearing out of nowhere, hopped right onto Boggs' shoulder.

"Most of the time, Curious stays in one of the famous window displays. But being a former circus monkey, she's trained and so I sometimes allow her to wander around the store before opening." Boggs considered the little monkey his own.

"He is adorable! Of course we will include him in the interview!"

"Are you excited to show Linda Langley and the rest of the world your store?" Boggs talked in baby language, petting the soft fur coat of the beloved store monkey.

Thirty minutes into the tour, Linda, being the reporter that she was, jumped right to the questions that she knew her public wanted answered. "So, Mr. Boggs, let's discuss the elephant in the room."

"Hey, how'd you know there's gonna be an elephant in the room?" Boggs couldn't believe what a great reporter Linda was. She knew things before they were announced to the public.

"Actually, I was referring to the damaging HeidtMoore headlines recently."

"Oh."

"So, tell me, do you expect any unforeseen incidents to happen? Do you feel prepared in case something—and I hate to say this—in case anything bad happens?"

"You kidding me? We got elephants! Let's go look at the space."

They arrived on the fifth floor, where the runway presentation would be in a couple of weeks.

Boggs was very proud to show off the vision for the Personal Appearance, showing Linda where the runway would be, where the VIP reception would take place and where the Instagrammable backdrops would be.

Suddenly Boggs noticed water trickling past Linda's feet. "Shoot! Not again."

Linda glanced down and jumped out of the way.

"We have a slight bathroom issue, Linda. Be right back," Boggs ran over to the men's bathroom where several engineers and housekeepers had cordoned off the space for repair work.

"Guys, you were here last week. Can't you get this fixed? We have a personal appearance coming up." He did not notice that Linda's crew was capturing every detail on camera.

Boggs returned to Linda and walked her away from the area. "Let's go visit the newly renovated spa," he said, hoping to leave her visit on a high note.

Event Meeting

Sloan arrived at work an hour early because of the excitement surrounding the personal appearance. He thought that he would be the first executive in the office and would have some time to plan in peace and quiet. However, as he approached the fifth floor, he noticed that Boggs was also early. Their eyes met and immediately appeared to race down the aisles in an attempt to outdo one another.

"Hi," said Sloan, with an uptight, pinched smile. "Thought you were on the late shift today?"

"Nah, got here bright and early. Crack of dawn. Already been for a run," Boggs replied, stretching his arms. "Only got in eight miles today."

As Boggs was talking, Sloan subconsciously tugged at his tight suit. *It never used to fit like this.* All of his suits were getting tighter and tighter. Only the middle button secured his jacket.

"I found out about the server issues and wanted to make sure it was getting fixed." Boggs continued.

"Oh? That's funny. I received all of my mail this morning." Sloan had gotten one up on Boggs.

"You did? When? How? Jeez."

"I just logged on."

They had reached the door to the executive offices. Sloan punched the keypad to unlock it. It didn't work.

"Here, I've got it." Boggs stepped up and punched in the code. The door opened immediately. "After you."

"No, go ahead." Sloan would not be humiliated.

◆

Within the hour, all of the managers involved in the personal appearance, which was basically the whole store, had gathered in the conference room to discuss the event happening the following week.

Vivian was determined to lead the meeting and began going over the list of requests.

"So, these are only some of the requests from Hudson Hawn. Keep in mind, this list is just for their greenroom, which we will use as the fur fitting room since it's the largest. They want the antique dressing tables from Sotheby's, new white carpet to be laid the morning of the event, only Moët & Chandon champagne... oh, and they are vegan. Chef, did you get the menu?"

"Yes, it's about ten pages long. I hope that ordering the food goes okay. Who has ever heard of spaghetti tofu?"

"What is in the huge packet?"

"Oh, that. That is the event setup and requests. Sloan and Boggs, you're handling that, right?"

They answered in unison. "Yes, we are."

Nacho coughed and then said, "Question. When will the guest list be complete? You know I have to do a check. After the active shooter, we don't want any Hudson Hawn stalkers to disrupt this thing."

"Great point, Nacho. I should have the complete list a couple of days before the event."

"Sloan, should we discuss the animal addition? I know that we discussed the elephant, but do we think that it's *wise*?" Vivian had added air quotes when saying the last word.

"It's going to be fantastic! The start of the event is an exciting HeidtMoore animal debut, followed by an opulent, eco-friendly runway show to showcase the Hudson Hawn line. Then, afterward, guests who have appointments with Goldie and Kate and will go to a designated area. And the rest... can shop!"

"Ok. But what about the elephant?"

"It's coming in next week from L.A." Ever since the PA had been announced, Sloan had been trying to secure something special for the show—the "wow" factor—and nothing would be more perfect than the stars of the show riding down the runway on an elephant.

"There's a list of requirements for the animal too."

"There is? Lord give me strength."

After the meeting had ended, the managers went over a quick review of their responsibilities for the day and what each of their presell goals were. Then they went back to the sales floor.

Olga's Agenda

With all of the personal appearance commotion going on in the store, Olga was finding more time to sneak off the sales floor to do what she did best: sell to coworkers. Every associate in the store, buying offices, and even the Online division knew Olga was the person to go to for a good deal. With her broken English and thick Russian accent, she made every product seem like the cheapest deal and very last one available.

"See, I have deal for you," Olga said to Brandi, catching her as she was heading to the ladies bathroom in the restaurant. "Come with me." Olga took Brandi to her secret nook in a back stairwell.

"Oh my gosh, Olga! where did you find these? I thought that they were sold out months ago!" Brandi tried on a pair of lime-green Miu Miu stilettos.

"I tell you I have deal. I have for you today."

"Yes, I want them. Just charge them. Oh, wait... I think that I have HeidtMoore Hundreds to use up. But you know you really shouldn't be selling things in the back hallway, Olga. It's store policy." Brandi felt slightly guilty for being somewhat complicit in Olga's unethical sales techniques.

"It is? Don't worry. I will ring for you and take to LP."

The guilt never lasted long. "Thank you, Olga! You're the best!" Brandi excitedly skipped up the stairs on her way to the restaurant.

♦

Olga went back out to the floor and over to her register to ring up the shoes for Brandi. As she was about to put the box of shoes in the bag, she noticed something sparkling near the side of the cash wrap. Upon closer inspection, she saw a magnificent quartz-and-emerald necklace. Olga had never seen anything so beautiful. The emeralds were the size of quarters and the quartz surrounding them was all dime-sized. It was probably worth thousands. *Is this real? Where did it come from?* Without any hesitation, she slyly cupped her hand over the necklace and slid it into the palm of her other hand just below the counter. She looked around to see if anyone was watching, then quickly put it in her pocket. Olga knew that this item could be exactly what she needed. She completed Brandi's transaction and while taking the shoes down to LP, made a stop back in the back hallway.

Olga carefully removed the necklace from her pocket and shoved it in a secret hole. Then she got on the phone.

"Oblensky. Oblensky. I have the money."

♦

Olga had not realized that Mary had been behind a rod of clothes next to her register, looking for an item for Mrs. Dinkleheimer. She had witnessed Olga looking around mysteriously. Once Olga left the floor, Mary went over to the register. She looked around the counter to see what Olga had been doing that had made Mary suspicious of her but there was nothing out of the ordinary. As Mary was about to leave, a little piece of plaster fell on her forehead. She looked up and saw a hole in the ceiling near the balcony. *Seriously, this place is really falling apart! Call the zookeeper.*

The Assessment Forms

It was another day... and another morning meeting. They were always much longer than they needed to be.

"What else is on the agenda? Boggs?" Sloan said.

"We are expanding the Handbag department for the 'I Have and You Don't' merchandise this week, in time for the Hudson Hawn event. There will also be a pop-up shop. I can't believe how popular those things are. My mom even wants one."

"We just got the huge shipment HH handbags. It will take until next week to go through it all," Tevi added in her characteristically drab tone.

Nacho was present at every meeting and it drove Mary a little crazy. He was so handsome. Always in charge and always confident and reassured.

"Please remind your associates about the closing procedures. We continue to find registers open and merchandise where it is not supposed to be. Remember guys, the cameras are everywhere." Nacho was one of the few managers who knew what was going on in the store. Mary had a question for Nacho.

"I do have a question about the associate assessment forms. Are they strictly for new hires, or tenured associates as well?" *Did he just?* He winked at her.

"All associates. The form is quick and it shouldn't take too long. I can help you after the meeting if you like, Mary?"

Mary blushed. "Thank you, Nacho."

Surprisingly, Boggs ended the meeting quicker than normal. "Okay, well that is all the time that we have today. Let's get back on the floor." Then pointed a finger at the managers. "Go get 'em, tigers!"

As Tevi, Mary, and Hilz walked out of the executive offices, they continued discussing the assessments.

"I guess I know what I will be doing this weekend. So much for movie night with my son. All my time goes to this job. I can't wait until these assessments are over."

The Men's manager continued, "I have a few associates who I'm concerned about. Margot, for example. She has been written up for so many things: chewing gum, wearing short skirts, putting on make-up in the morning as if this place were her bathroom. I swear, she 'tests' every bit of makeup and fragrance that we have... and on top of that, she stockpiles the samples. It's not even her home base department! She sells suits for a living."

Tevi agreed. "Oh, I know. I have one who still refuses to step out of the Handbag department. She doesn't have any knowledge of cosmetics or shoes. Yet complains that her sales are down. I have to flag her for that on the form. And don't get me started on bloody Sparkle! The one time that she steps out of the department, she causes the biggest embarrassment. I've never been so disgusted in my life. The Gottrocks luncheon! Unbelievable."

"Oh yeah, we heard about that."

"Fuck. I guess I will be working on that this weekend. I should just mark them all fail. All of they do is bitch and cry and then bitch some more."

♦

Once Tevi was in the Cosmetics department, she stopped by Glamzone Glow, the only $5-million-dollar counter on the floor. The line carried every plumping cosmetic imaginable: lipstick, foundation, hair serum, and bottom plumper.

"So, where are we today?" Tevi spotted the counter manager applying lip plumper and primping herself instead of taking care of the clients who were milling about the floor.

"What do you mean?" She put down her plumper and handheld mirror.

"How much do you have in? What is your goal? Come on, we don't have all day."

"The goal is ten. I have in, um...."

"How much?" Tevi demanded.

"I have in two. Maybe."

"Maybe? $2,000? Get a move on! I'm reporting all numbers to Corporate today. How are you going to report $2,000 to the bigwigs when they come in at 2:00pm?"

"It will change by then."

"Bloody useless. How about you worry less about your appearance and worry more about how you think you are going to make your numbers." Then, she had one final jab. "This counter. It is filthy. Did you clean the counter?"

The associate was almost in tears. *Why was Tevi such a bitch? It wasn't fair!*

Distracting Tevi from berating her associate was Nacho, who had been strolling the floor, occasionally chatting to a sales person, and making sure that everything was in check. "Hey, Nacho. Call one of your housekeeping guys. This counter is gross."

Nacho took this as an order to approach the Glamzone Glow counter. "It looks fine to me."

"No. It's gross. See this? Dust! Gross," she said dismissively before sauntering off to another counter, like a drill sergeant, demanding more presell numbers.

"Anything you say." Giving Tevi an army salute, He turned to the embarrassed associate standing there, her lips progressively getting plumper, and wondered if the other products sold just as well. He held up a bottom plumper. "So, you sell many of these?"

◆

While Nacho was on his daily security check, walking through the store, he happened to find himself in the Children's department. He saw Mary at a distance doing her job, picking up after kids and talking to everyone, seeing to their every need. He was impressed by how well she handled one mother berating her for not having the latest Dolce & Gabbana diaper bag. He noticed how calmly she managed the chaos of the children running around while simultaneously making sure that her merchandise was fully stocked and her lazy associates were doing their jobs.

How could he ask her out again without anyone finding out? Or risk her getting lockjaw? *Not to a bar, I guess.* Perhaps the moment was now. No associates were watching and she was busy dealing with a toddler who had shoved another child into the baby grand piano. *Typical.*

He approached the register where she had previously been ringing up some items for a customer and wrote her a note: *Come join me for lunch today. My treat! Anything you like. See you in the Café at 2. Anything comes up, text me. Nacho.*

He slipped the note into an envelope and labeled it "Mary." Then he walked away. He couldn't wait to see her again.

◆

A while after Nacho had left the department, Mary was called away to her office and never got back to the register to finish her presell strategy. Instead, Ethel came over with a mound of children's sale items that she was ringing up for Olga. Dumping them on the register, she hadn't seen the envelope and missed the note falling to the floor.

♦

It was 2:15pm and Nacho was waiting at a table in the Café. He continued to wait but Mary never arrived.

Hudson Hawn PA

The day had come. Every associate was excited about the prospect of meeting the huge celebrities of Hudson Hawn. They were also excited about the prospect of making a lot of money. There were still a few details to be worked out though. For instance, the shipment of the Hudson Hawn fall line of probiotic-infused organic onesies, the ones that *Vogue* had featured in its September issue. These onesies were the must-have items that everyone needed, as they made every woman, man, child, and pet, regardless of shape, look absolutely fabulous. The magazine explicitly told the reader that the product could only be found at the HeidtMoore, so the store had been inundated with calls. T kept a list in the office that had already exceeded a thousand names.

"Bro'," said Boggs to Willy, who was ticketing some bondage sticks that had arrived for the Intimates department. "We gotta get this merchandise, man. Ever since that bag, I'm not taking any chances." Willy threw up his hands, dropping the sticks. "Boggs, I don't know what to tell you. They were supposed to be here with a noon delivery. Maybe the one o'clock shipment will have it. We have the afternoon and the event isn't until this evening. The Lady Gaga *"Born This Way"* ringtone sounded.

"This is Boggs. Hello?" *Oh dear. It was PR.*

"I need to know how many pieces in the onesie shipment. The Hudson Hawn team wants a number and a presell amount. Like, right now."

"Hey Viv, it's cool. Not in the noon shipment. But Willy assures me," he said, glancing over at Willy with a knowing look in his eye, "that it will be here with the one o'clock shipment." Willy gave Boggs a sarcastic smile.

On the fifth floor, the Whole World, the choice vendor for the store, had arrived to set up that morning. They brought in two hundred Chiavari chairs, a gold foiled runway and a lighting setup for the show. Behind the scenes, Vivian, her assistant and Sloan were going through the racks of clothing to be shown on the runway.

"Do we have Men's?"

"Yes." Sloan began responding to each question on her list.

"Women's?"

"Yes"

"What about Children's?"

"Got it."

"Handbags, Shoes and Jewelry?

"All check."

"Now this is what is going to happen. The elephant is coming at the end of the Hudson Hawn appearance. Then, Sloan, you will close out the show with a few words since Mr. Heidt won't be here. Yet again."

Sloan was clapping his hands like a seal with excitement. Vivian felt like all he needed was a beach ball on his nose to complete this one-man show. Vivian hoped that the elephant would behave, unlike the days prior, when the practice didn't go as planned... in part because Pietro was trying to take charge.

◆

"Okay, everybody. We want *every* associate lined up on both sides. So that we have a certain number *here*," Pietro said dramatically, pointing to one side of the runway, and then to the other, "and a certain number *here*."

When the group of associates didn't move immediately, Pietro physically started to move people, as if they were pieces of furniture in a staged play. Then he scurried behind the partition to check something. He ran back to the end of the runway and began the countdown.

"Now, on the count of three, when you see the special guest arrive, I want you all to start clapping. Now of course the special guest won't actually be here until the event, so we currently have someone else filling in."

"I'm a celebrity!" shouted one of the associates. Pietro ignored the comment.

"We'll just have to deal with Sloan. Use your imagination. One... two... three!" He pulled the red velvet curtain open, revealing Sloan on top of a giant elephant. Everyone started clapping in awe and amazement at the spectacle. After a few moments, the clapping died down and the elephant remained immobile.

"Come on... Come on...." Sloan gently nudged the elephant. Sloan's face suddenly became beet red. The elephant was constipated. "Oh no, can someone get me off of this thing?"

Viv stepped up to the elephant. "No. That's not part of the show. Get on with it."

"No. *Now.* I must get off of this thing." He felt the elephant's sides rumble and his tail suddenly rise up. There were collective gasps from the audience.

"The bloody elephant is taking a shit!" Tevi was pushed out of the way by Pietro, who was trying not to hyperventilate.

"No. No! Not on the Venetian marble floor!"

Meanwhile, Curious, who had quietly snuck in, was strutting down the runway clapping. This was a practice session that everyone wanted to forget.

◆

Vivian stood there in the space, calculating the number of seats, models, runway stability, and lighting scheme. She took a deep breath. *Only three hours until showtime.*

Across the way, Boggs was on the sales floor.

"So, Mer, how are we doing with presell?" Boggs said. Mary was taken by surprise as she was in the middle of coaching Lulu on the new selling app, "HeidtMoore Buy More."

"Hi, Boggs. I was just showing Lulu the stalking feature on the app. Give me just a moment," Mary said, turning back to give Lulu her full attention. "You see, you just touch this button and you can see everything that your customer has been browsing online."

"Oh, thank you very much, Mary." Lulu wandered off to practice. Mary turned to Boggs. "It has been very hard to sell without the product. Are they here yet?"

"Not here Mer, but they are arriving any minute now." *It was the same old story again.* "But Boggs, no one is willing to commit without actually seeing the product."

"Now Mary, you know that is an excuse. You've been here for months now, you should know better than that."

Mary hated it when Boggs patronized her. "I understand. Have any of the onesies come in for any of the other departments?" Before storming off, Boggs replied, "No onesies in Women's. No onesies in Men's. Not one onesie!" That ended that conversation.

◆

Pietro was not happy at all. He could not stand that the Whole World was coming into his world.

"No, no, no, noooo," he said, pointing to the spotlights. He did not like that he was not in charge of the runway visual. Yet he was still trying to take control. "Yes, that's right! Make sure that this entire area is flooded with light. The models will each stop here and spin." He mimicked the catwalk stance and then spun around dramatically. After a couple of test runs, he was satisfied and left the runway. *I hope that we do not have another blackout. The lighting is everything!*

♦

Chef popped his head into HR. "Hey, got time for a quickie?" Brandi replied with a giggle, "You nasty boy... you should be getting ready for the event. Don't you have cream tarts to make?" He shut the door behind him and replied, "I have a special cream tart for you."

♦

Back in the kitchen, it was absolute mayhem. The signature air-puff muffins were burning in the oven. To add to the chaos, the entire batch of orange spiced tea was having to be remade. Someone had accidentally added vodka to the entire thing instead of only to the VIP selection. While Chef had left the kitchen, the sous chef and two of the line cooks had taken the opportunity to go outside for a smoke break.

♦

Hudson Hawn was due to arrive any moment. Vivian paced nervously by the VIP entrance. She was also on edge about the budget. Since the event had started, the PR department had accrued $25,000 in additional expenses. Vivian's cell phone rang. It was the Hudson Hawn team.

"Hey! This is Kayla, the point person at Hudson Hawn. Just checking in with you. Goldie and Kate are running a little late. They we be delayed another hour or so. Okay, bye."

"Not a problem. Okay, bye," replied Vivian. A giant lie. *Great. There goes another $200 in limo fare.*

Elsewhere in the store, everything looked magnificent. It was all set for the personal appearance. The marble floors were scrubbed clean and the counters polished to perfection. Every gold pillar and even the cylindrical fish tank in the center of the store had Hudson Hawn welcome signs.

Guests started to arrive and were dressed exclusively head-to-toe in Hudson Hawn. Nacho was walking through the store. In each department, he paused to speak into his walkie-talkie, confirming coverage with Danny and Brad, who were overseeing the cameras.

A velvet rope sectioned off half of the fourth floor. A line of VIP guests and spectators were eagerly awaiting entry into the runway seating area.

Sloan was busy mingling with the guests in the line and hoping to take a bite or two of the hors d'oeuvres. That's when he realized that they weren't being passed. He saw Mary observing her floor and motioned to her. She wanted to ignore him but couldn't.

"Yes?" She walked over to him. He asked Mary where the waiters were, as if she were in charge of the event. "I'm not sure, I'll go find Chef."

Quickly walking out to the back hall to the kitchen, Mary spied Chef coming around the corner, appearing to have rushed from the restroom."

"Chef. Chef!" Mary yelled to get his attention.

"Yes, Mary?"

"The hors d'oeuvres are not being passed yet."

"Let me get to the kitchen and see what is going on."

Chef arrived in the kitchen to discover that a new batch of air-puff muffins just coming out of the oven. "What the hell! These should have been done already."

◆

Moments later, attractive shirtless waiters hovered around the fourth floor passing out the air-puff muffins and the Hudson Hawn cocktail: a vegan, grass-fed, non-GMO, nonfat, sugar-free, paleo-infused, nonalcoholic cherry spritzer, all served with an avocado garnish.

More and more guests were arriving. Backstage, the models were waiting for instructions from Vivian and Pietro. Every element was in place except for the onesies.

"Willy, I can't get ahold of Boggs. Where the heck are the onesies? The show starts in ten minutes!"

◆

Boom! Boom! Boom!

The music started. The bass drum kicked in. It was a mixture of tribal music and spiritual meditation music. Customers couldn't help but sway to the rhythmic sound of the infectious beats coming from the deejay booth located next to the runway.

The lights dimmed, except for the spotlighting on the runway.

Sloan held his breath.

All of the guests were seated. The catwalk shimmered. Everything seemed magical. Vivian previewed one side of the crowd. She saw Mrs.

Gottrocks all bejeweled in the front row. Seated next to her were Mr. and Mrs. Dinkleheimer. A couple of rows back, Linda Langley was busy taking notes in her notebook. Vivian scanned the other side of the room and noticed a group of associates as well as Tevi, Sparkle, Olga, and Lulu. Brandi, with champagne flute in hand, came up to Vivian.

"Good luck, Vivian! It's going to be great. So exciting!" Brandi teetered off to find a place to watch the show.

T ran over to Vivian, "Oh my God. I just got a call from Willy. Several boxes of the onesies fell off the truck."

"What! My God, T... well, tell him to bring them up immediately. We have got to have them now. The show starts in five minutes." T ran down the back stairs to the Shipping and Receiving department, where a dozen or so panicked OST team members were frantically counting damaged boxes.

"My God! What happened!?"

"Well, the funniest thing. The boxes were delivered at noon... to the store zoo food-container area. Somehow they got mixed up with the regular pallets of food."

♦

Vivian, with her headset on, motioned to Pietro. "Models ready." He gave her the thumbs up.

Moving to the side from behind the partition, the first model appeared. The model stood for a brief moment, then proceeded to walk down the runway. Boggs, watching from the side, thought she looked more like a speeding giraffe than any normal-looking human being. Each of the models thereafter held her head high, always poised and focused, with long legs strident and in control of her delicate frame. The clothes only enhanced their incredible beauty. One after another, the models walked back and forth. The luxurious satins, velvets and lace from the Hudson Hawn line made the clothes look exquisite. Then came the Men's line. Each male model was chiseled like a Roman god. It didn't matter that they were wearing tartan pants and polka dot shirts under faux-fur vests layered with chenille Cloak and Dagger-type coats.

Some models had live animals with them, from parrots and iguanas to sloths and llamas. Even the animals had couture outfits and jewelry. The final group to strut the catwalk was a family of four, each member debuting the much-anticipated onesies. T had helped Willy bring the merchandise upstairs just as the show began.

"What about the kids, how are they going to get in these?" At that moment, a team of seamstresses were sewing the children right into the onesies without a hitch. Then off they went, down the runway to rapturous applause from the crowd.

That was it! Ninety looks in thirty minutes. Sloan breathed a sigh of relief and the crowd erupted into applause. Kate and Goldie came out on the elephant for the ending, blew kisses to the crowd and were led back behind the curtain.

Breaking News

The day after the personal appearance Nacho arrived early to walk the store before opening. There had been a late night of celebrating. It was a giant success; the stress and drama had all paid off.

"Man, what a night last night. Are all of the cameras up? We need to walk the floor."

◆

"Good morning, team!" Boggs was going to lead his team of managers and get the day rolling. That was, until Sloan walked in.

"Good morning, everyone."

No one said a word. As if nothing had happened, Boggs continued with his morning rally. Every department manager had gathered in the executive offices.

"As you have probably heard, everyone was thrilled with the show and our sales exceeded expectations. Hudson Hawn sold $500,000 in one day!" Everyone clapped and no none was more pleased—or relieved—than Vivian, who was with the group of managers.

"And this means that we made our month!" Sloan interjected, always having to have the last word.

"Thank you, Sloan." Boggs tried hard to be polite. "I just got off the phone with IT and they have assured me that we will be back up and running by noon. Until then, if anything is urgent, we will text you. Now, as we start the week it is imperative that we hit the goals set for the promotion. Mr. Heidt will be back from his trip soon and we do not want him to be disappointed."

◆

In the back of the room, none of the managers were paying any attention to Boggs. Or Sloan.

Tevi was busy eating a banana nut loaf. *How am I going to stop Sparkle from crying this time? Hey, what is she drinking? I want some.*

Mary didn't see Tevi's eagle eyes fall on her double mocha latte. *This is so fattening, yet delicious. I need to go on a diet.*

Sarafina was thrilled to have her luncheon over with. It had been a success and now on to other important things. *Who makes her shoes? I must have them. Better than those godforsaken Moonboots.* She was referring to Judith, an assistant selling manager who was, unlike Sarafina, restless and ready to get out of the room.

Judith, a short, feisty Jewish woman in her early fifties, had worked at the HeidtMoore in various capacities since the 1970s. *Oh for God's sake. Let's get this meeting over with and let me talk about these damn Moonboots. So over them. Enough already.*

Brandi was present for every manager meeting, along with her Yeti flask. *What is it about him? I cannot handle it. Why does he have to be SO H.O.T?* She was, of course, looking at Chef.

Chef liked to use this manager meeting as an opportunity to talk about the specials and to flirt with Brandi. He smiled at her seductively. *God, I want to rip her shirt off and play with those big bouncing—*

"Chef. Hello, Chef?" He was concentrating so hard on Brandi that he hadn't heard Boggs ask him about the daily specials.

"Huh? Excuse me. What?"

"Chef, you're going to send out the updates to the new menu and additional items to the spring menu, correct?" Boggs did not like Chef and he didn't mind making it known.

"Loud and clear. I expect I will get it up." Brandi went bright red and tried to hide behind her Yeti flask. Chef corrected himself.

"I mean... send it out."

"Okay, any other announcements? Betty, what about you?"

Betty, the Gift Galleries coordinator was a lovely people-pleaser with only one flaw: her tendency to drool when she got excited or nervous. Mary gave her a gentle push for encouragement.

"We are having our annual 'Scent Fest' this week and the candles are exclusive to our store. They sell for $1,500. We have presold a dozen already but still have a way to go. There is an email available so please remind your associates to send it out to their clients." She looked back at Mary for approval. Mary smiled and motioned to Betty to wipe the drool off of her lip.

"Very nice, Betty. Good job. Very nice. Anyone else? Becks. Whacha got?"

Becks, was a loud, outspoken, overweight, and overbearing buyer from Corporate. She had been placed in the Contemporary department to stand in for the existing manager, who had taken a leave of absence following the active shooter. Becks had been dying to talk the whole time.

"This week for the promotion we have new JBrand jeans. *WOOOO!!!* They just rolled out size 000... yes, triple zero. So my big toe will fit into that. Oh, also, since I'm on the Customer Service Committee, don't forget 11-4 on the floor."

Where did she come from? She is going to be the biggest pain in my ass. Tevi couldn't stand the smug know-it-alls from Corporate.

"Thanks, Becks. Welcome to the team. Anyone else?"

"Moonboots! Moonboots! Moonboots! These are the trendiest shoes right now. I can't believe it. They are big and bulky and silver, and we have lots to sell. Please have your associates come to the department and show their clients."

"Yep. Guys, everyone needs a pair. Do they make a size 13?" No one said a word. "Okay, any other announcements?"

Silence. "Okay, well everyone have—"

"Wait. One more thing. Please check your schedules for Thursday. The Vice President will be in the store and will want a walk through. We will send out an itinerary shortly." Sloan was pleased to close out the meeting with this tidbit of information.

"Really? You got this information?"

"Yes Boggs, I got this information! Okay, thanks everyone. Make it an opulent day!" The managers proceeded to file out of the room, leaving only Boggs and Sloan to glare at one another.

♦

As Nacho was leaving the office, he saw Mary coming in through the employee doors, Starbucks in one hand and file folders in the other. *Organized.* He liked that about her. He caught her eye and felt the urge to flex a bicep. Mary smiled and blushed ever so slightly.

Just as he was about to walk over to her, now confident that he could confront her about standing him up at lunch, he got a call on his cell phone.

"Yes. Okay, I'm headed down now. Do *not* open the doors until I say so."

♦

In front of the store, Laura Langley and her news crew had set up her filming station.

"Hello, we are reporting live from the most magnificent department store in the country. For years the HeidtMoore has set the standard for the finest-quality merchandise, displayed for the most distinguished, high net-worth customers to purchase... and for the rest of the world to gaze at. With Apple's latest release of the iShop4, customers are no longer shopping at the so-called Museum of Merchandise, here at the HeidtMoore. Or are they?"

What on earth was she doing here? Nacho did not need to be dealing with reporters at this early hour. It was ridiculous. Hadn't she done enough reporting on the store after everything that had happened?

Nacho walked out to hear the last of the news report.

"Excuse me. We are opening soon. Is there something that I can help you with?"

"We are just finishing up. But since you are here, may I ask you a couple of questions?" Linda Langley had caught a big fish; now it was time to real him in. "Just one question?" She said batting her eyelids.

"Our PR team handles all interviews. I'm in charge of Security." For extra emphasis, Nacho puffed out his chest.

"Security? Well, I guess that you have heard the news then?"

"What news?"

"The HeidtMoore is closing and Mr. Heidt has been found... dead."

Nacho stood there, stunned. "We are opening now, so if you will excuse me." At that moment Brad rushed out.

"Sorry, sir. But I need to let you know that we found the necklace."

Want to find out what happens to the employees of the HeidtMoore during its busiest holiday season ever? Will a retail collaboration save the store's reputation... or destroy it? Will new technology prove to be more of a hindrance than a help? Will employee turnover be a blessing or a nightmare? And for Mary and Nacho, will their relationship status make it to *#love*?

Stay tuned for our exciting next installment in the HeidtMoore series:

Online or Off

#heidtmoore

Made in the USA
Columbia, SC
26 May 2019